W9-ADC-815

PRINCE PUGGLY
OF SPUD
AND THE KINGDOM OF SPIFF

PRINCE PUGGLY
OF SPUD
AND THE KINGDOM OF SPIFF

robert paul weston

PUFFIN

an imprint of Penguin Canada

Published by the Penguin Group

Penguin Group (Canada), 90 Eglinton Avenue East, Suite 700, Toronto, Ontario, Canada M4P 2Y3

Penguin Group (USA) Inc., 375 Hudson Street, New York, New York 10014, U.S.A.
Penguin Books Ltd, 80 Strand, London WC2R 0RL, England
Penguin Ireland, 25 St Stephen's Green, Dublin 2, Ireland (a division of Penguin Books Ltd)
Penguin Group (Australia), 707 Collins Street, Melbourne, Victoria 3008, Australia
(a division of Pearson Australia Group Pty Ltd)
Penguin Books India Pvt Ltd, 11 Community Centre, Panchsheel Park, New Delhi – 110 017, India
Penguin Group (NZ), 67 Apollo Drive, Rosedale, Auckland 0632, New Zealand
(a division of Pearson New Zealand Ltd)
Penguin Books (South Africa) (Pty) Ltd, 24 Sturdee Avenue, Rosebank,
Johannesburg 2196, South Africa

Penguin Books Ltd, Registered Offices: 80 Strand, London WC2R 0RL, England

Published in Puffin hardcover by Penguin Canada, 2013
Simultaneously published in the United States by Penguin Young Readers Group

1 2 3 4 5 6 7 8 9 10 (RRD)

Copyright © Robert Paul Weston, 2013

Book design by Kristin Smith
Illustrations by Víctor Rivas Villa

Manufactured in the U.S.A.

ISBN: 978-0-670-06397-0

Library and Archives Canada Cataloguing in Publication data available upon request to the publisher.
American Library of Congress Cataloging in Publication data available.

Visit the Penguin Canada website at www.penguin.ca

Special and corporate bulk purchase rates available;
please see **www.penguin.ca/corporatesales** or call 1-800-810-3104, ext. 2477.

ALWAYS LEARNING   **PEARSON**

For Machiko

"Why, my esteemed sire, I am merely feeding the true guest of honor at this banquet . . . my cloak!"

—Mulla Nasruddin

CHAPTER 1
a Kingdom of Taste

Once,
long ago,
in a faraway land,
there rose up a palace
stupendously grand.

It was built by the sea, on the rim of a cliff,
on the easternmost edge of the

KINGDOM OF SPIFF.

Through the doors you could see a magnificent stair.
It went spiraling gracefully into the air.
Beyond it were hallways that

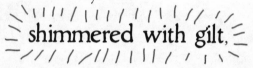

shimmered with gilt,

for that's how a Spiffian palace was built.

Every inch was luxurious, posh without fail.
It was utterly stylish in every detail:
from faucets that *s p a r k l e d* with glittering gems,

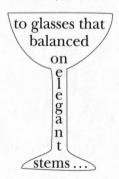

to glasses that
balanced
on
e
l
e
g
a
n
t
stems …

Spiff, after all, was a kingdom of taste,
where following fashion was fully embraced;
and nowhere was fashion in evidence more
than in

clothes —of the

sort that the Spiffians wore.

This was a kingdom that dressed to the *NINES*,
where everyone sported the latest designs.

leap up

They would ⁓ like lemmings to follow a craze.
They were (x x / victims) of fashion ... in all the worst ways.

Every Spiff in the land would compete with their friends,
to keep right in step with the latest of trends.
They always were wearing the sassiest styles
(which of course they would sport with the
smuggest of smiles).

There was only one person in all of the land
for whom **"fashion"** was something she just
couldn't stand.

That person was

Frannie,

THE PRINCESS OF SPIFF,

who lived in the castle, on the edge of that cliff.

Frannie, you see . . . well, she just didn't care.
She rarely dressed up or embellished her hair.
She never wore dresses or elegant coats.

She wore only
pajamas.
They were printed
with boats.

Each morning, the princess would roll out of bed,
with a scandal of hair

b l a z i n g   u p

from her head.
She would plod down the hallways of silver and gold
to the ballroom, which was always a sight to behold.

It wasn't just any old ballroom, you see.
This one was "***THE BEST!***" (by official decree).
"**THE BIGGEST**." "THE BRIGHTEST."
"THE FINEST OF ALL."
For this was none other than

Frolicsome Hall!

Its ivory walls were creamy and bright!
The chandeliers practically *trembled* with light!
The ceiling was pitched in a sumptuous dome,
and this, in a way, was the princess's home.

On the floor she had cushions, piled up in a heap,

both incredibly high and incredibly steep.

It went up to the rafters! It was terribly high!
Were it piled out of doors it would puncture the sky!

Each morning, Francesca would climb to the top.
She'd bring up a book, and there she would plop.
Then page after page, on her plushy plateau,
she would read some old Austen, some Dickens
or Poe.

To her father, however, this was nearly a sin.
He regarded his daughter with a look of chagrin . . .

"*Francesca,*" he grumbled, "you cannot be here.
We'll be needing this room on next Saturday, dear.
Surely you know: This is Frolicsome Hall!

*It is here we shall hold our
Centenary Ball!"*
(Her father, you see, was King Dandy von Fop.
In fashion, the man was the cream of the crop.)

Frannie just shrugged. "No problem," she said.
"You can dance round my pillows. You go right ahead.

You can do what you like, get all fancily dressed,
then have your '*soiree.*'
I don't mind.
Be my guest."

"Oh, Frannie," her elegant father replied.
For one quiet moment, he stood there and sighed.
"It's not only your pillows, but also your clothes.
Pajamas? I can't have you dressing in those!

"Now, I know," he went on, while fluffing his wig,
"you may think I'm a snob, or a bit of a prig,
but *really*, Francesca, just look at you there.
Isn't there *anything* else you could wear?"

And so, the king's message was clearly conveyed.
The princess, however, was hard to persuade.
"Oh, Daddy," she answered, "why can't you see?
We're different—*completely*. We'll never agree."

"I can try," said the king. "I mean, look how you're dressed!
Pajamas?!

My dear, is that really your best?
It's quite unbecoming, to tell you the truth.
I might go so far as to call it '**UNCOUTH**.'

"It's clear that I know what I'm talking about.
At the altar of fashion, I'm fairly devout.
As you know very well, I'm so hip that it hurts.
My pants are like heaven—and so are my shirts.

"So dress more like me! I'm the **KING**, after all.
Not to mention, your father, as I'm sure you recall."
But Francesca von Fop had a mind of her own

(something King Dandy should really have known).

"I'm sorry," said Frannie. "That isn't my thing,
and please—don't remind me that you are 'the king.'
I'm aware of all that, but I'd rather just read.
My books and my cushions are all that I need."

"Perhaps ... " the king muttered. "But listen, for once.
You've been lying up there, just reading, for *months*!
With the PARTY this weekend," he said, with a frown,
"it's time to get dressed.

It's

time

to

come

down."

It was true. On the eve of that Saturday night,
the kingdom would be a remarkable sight!
Every footpath and fountain, every garden and gate,
would be fancy and spangled and *oh, so ornate*!

The guests would arrive. They would

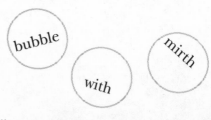

bubble

with

mirth

They would kick up their heels, for all they were worth!

They would come for the Spiffian *Glamour*

and *Glitz!*

The FASHION, REFINEMENT!

The RAZZLE and RITZ!

"So you see," said the king to his daughter above,
"I make this request out of nothing but love.
Every kingdom for leagues, they all know about this.
It's the one night that nobody wishes to miss!

"They *all* want an invite. They're begging for one!

Every monarch for miles wants a piece of the fun.

What they want is to mingle, to *see and be seen*.
This is SPIFF, after all. Do you see what I mean?

"What will they think, with you lounging up there?
In pajamas! With boats!
(Not to mention your hair.)
These are princes and queens,
from f   a   r and from **wide**.
They'll call you a *schlub*. It's a matter of pride.

"And what about me? They'll think I'm a *schnook*
when they see you, just lying there, reading a book.
So what would you say to a dress with a bow?
A necklace, perhaps, or a little chapeau?"

"I'd say NO!" Frannie cried.

"You don't like how I dress?
Then you'll just have to cancel your *PARTY*, I guess!
Now leave me," she said, from her cushiony roost.

"I'm right in the middle of reading my Proust!"

CHAPTER 2
a Chink in the Chain of Command

Meanwhile,
nearby in the kingdom next door
was a castle not known for its lofty décor.
It hardly was flashy or fancy or grand.
Compared to its neighbors, this palace was **bland**.

Unlike the Spiffians' castle of GLASS,
this palace was built out of copper and brass.
There were zig zags and STRIPES on every last wall,
and only one turret. One turret, that's all!

For this was none other than the

KiNGDOM OF SPUD,

a kingdom that mostly was covered in mud.

There had once been a king.
He'd been handsome and chic,
but in Spud, being chic made you seem like a freak.
His name was King Walter . . . but it didn't work out.
Ever since he was young, he had wrestled with doubt.

After all, the Spudlian manner of dress
was perhaps best described as . . . *willful excess.*
For instance, their wigs were all ropy and rough,

fluff.

of

like violent volcanic eruptions

In Spiff, every hairpiece was natty and neat,
while in Spud? They seemed to be scraped off the street.
On their scalps, it looked like a jungle had bloomed.
But that's how they liked it.
It's how they were groomed.

So too with their clothes; they could never be missed.
For a Spudlian outfit would often consist
of POLKA-DOT trousers,
a CHECKERED chemise,
with *tiger-print patches* on the elbows and knees.

That was Spudlian clothing. So GARISH! So LOUD!
But they *liked* it that way. In fact, they were proud.
Although some might call it grotesque or absurd,
it was simply what Spudlian people preferred.

To them, it was stylish; it was simply the trend.
(We'll call it "eccentric," so as not to offend.)

Yet somehow the king thought this fashion was bad.
With his people in paisley and bright-yellow plaid,
he began to suspect that he didn't belong,
that being a Spud—well, it simply felt *wrong*.

He believed this was true, in his bones, in his blood,
so he went to consult with:
THE SHAMAN OF SPUD ...

Ah, yes! The Shaman! That preacher of peace!
In his billowy, bell-bottomed breeches of fleece!
With his glasses as thick as the base of a jar,
the lens for each eye in the shape of a star!

With his bristling goatee! His flowery robes!
The jingle of earrings on both of his lobes!
His dreadlocks that hung like the strings on a mop,
and his fluffy red turban ... with a daisy on top!

THE SHAMAN OF SPUD was a mystic, a seer.
He lived in a hut, to the palace's rear,
subsisting on nothing but yogurt and rice,
which is why you went there, when you needed advice.

"Uh, Shaman?" said the king, stepping into the hut.
"I've got this bad feeling, deep down in my gut."
He explained how he felt, with a pitiful pout.
"I just don't fit in. I'm the oddest man out.
The problem is simple: *I can't stand my clothes!*

They certainly aren't the ones I would have chose.

"I want something *regal*, something worthy of praise!
Have you seen what they're wearing in Spiff nowadays?

FASHION with *elegance*, *Glamour*
and *Glitz!*

FASHION that matches—and actually fits!

"That's nothing like us. Our clothes are a sham.
This kingdom would fail any fashion exam!
I'm serious, Shaman. This kingdom would *flunk*.
Surely you've noticed. We dress like we're *drunk*."

All the while, as King Walter continued to gripe,
the Shaman just sat there and puffed on his pipe.
Then, when King Walter's complaints were complete,

the Shaman of Spud floated up to his feet.

"**Dude**," said the Shaman. "You gotta relax.
You're the king of the Spuds—and those are the facts.
Do you know what it means to be 'Spudly,' my man?
It means you dress up just as **wild** as you can!

"Look at me here. Check out these threads.
I look *gooood*—from my shoes to my velvety dreads!
These clothes are not 'clothes.' These clothes are *an art!*
We Spuds wear 'em **wild**. It's what sets us apart.

"Our Spudlian duds are the grooviest rags!
We got **CHECKERS** and P O L K A - D O T S,
ZIGGLES and *ZAGS!*
To be 'Spudly,' my man? It means crazy-with-zest!
Dude! It's how Spudlian people look best."

Having finished his speech, full of bluster and hype,
the Shaman sank back to the floor, with his pipe.

To King Walter, however, the Shaman's advice
wasn't very much help. It would never suffice
to make him feel better, or any less tense.
To him, the whole speech hadn't made any sense.

"Uh . . . thanks," said the king, backing out of the hut.
In his mind, he was thinking: *That Shaman's a nut.*

The very next morning, in the faintness of dawn,
King Walter walked out on the palace's lawn.
ONLY HALF OF THE KINGDOM / WAS EVEN AWAKE
when he said that he had an announcement to make.

"My people!" he cried. "This kingdom's a dud!
It's clear I'm too cool for the **Kingdom of SPUD**.
If I stay, I shall always be misunderstood.
So henceforth, and forthwith, I'm leaving for good."

Then he colored his hair, he bought some new clothes,
and he hired a surgeon to alter his nose.

(Lately, I've heard that he calls himself "Chip,"
and runs a salon in the Kingdom of Hip.)

Anyway, getting back to the story at hand,
there now was a chink in the chain of command.
The kingdom was kingless! The Spuds were alone!
There was nary a bum in the seat of the throne!

Having been callously left in the lurch,
the Spudlian people went off on a search
for someone who wouldn't go *r u n n i n g* away,
who wasn't "too cool," who'd be willing to stay.

What they wanted was someone with clothing that
CLAshED,
ill-fitting clothing that **DAZZLED** and *FLASHED!*
A model of Spud, who would charm and beguile,
with the wildness and weirdness of Spudlian style!

A **SPUD** among **SPUDS!** A person who wore
clothes any Spud in the world would *adore!*

So bands of explorers set gallantly forth,
to the icebergs of **mud** in the Spudlian north,
to the south, where the **mud** was the color of fudge,
to the east, where it flowed in a slithery sludge.

Some even went west, to the **mud**-covered moors
(where **mud** was so common, it was even indoors),
and there, in the miry muck of the west,
they found a young man who was suitably dressed.

They discovered a ramshackle wreck of a shed.
The building looked *SICK*...

OR DYING...

OR DEAD.

It was crooked and faded and grubby and SMALL,
with mold growing over each withering wall.

The shack was a ruin, an utter disgrace!
Could anyone live in so wretched a place?
In a home full of mildew and festering rot?
The answer was: *Yes, believe it or not.*

PUGGLY
O'BUNGLETON,

that was his name,
a common young man of no worldly acclaim.

When he answered the door, every Spud felt a CHILL.
They stood there, just staring. THEY STOOD VERY STILL.
They knew by his shirt and they knew by his pants,
they knew in an instant, with only a glance . . .

He's perfect! they thought. It's just as we planned.
He's the Spudliest dresser in all of the land!
And so THEY JUST STOOD THERE, agape and aghast.
It was clear they had found their new leader at last.

Indeed, it was true. This boy was ideal.
He had just the right sort of unstylish appeal.
To be frank, his clothing was rather a fright.
His socks were too loose, yet his sleeves were too tight.

And the colors! So many had come to collide,
it looked like a beautiful rainbow—had died.
These colors were **wild**. He looked like a clown!
Orange and purple and yellow and brown!

The explorers, however, were duly impressed.
They thought the young man was quite sensibly dressed.
This was beautiful, classical, Spudlian fare!
And so they explained to him why they were there ...

"W-wait," Puggly stammered, when they were through.
"You want *me?* As your king?! To *lead* all of you?"
Wide-eyed, he gaped at the crowd at his door,
their trousers besmeared with the mud of the moor.

"Well, actually ... *no,*" said a Spud at the front.
"*Kings* aren't the best, to be perfectly blunt."

"It's true," said another. "We care not for kings!
They're fickle, capricious, unreliable things!
They run off to be *barbers,*" he went on, with a wince.
"We don't want a king. What we *need*—is a

PRINCE."

Puggly said nothing. His face had gone pale.
His sense of surprise? It was right off the scale.

PRINCE?! the boy thought. No, I must have misheard.
Me? As a prince?! Why, that's just absurd.
I must be mistaken. They didn't say "prince."
I'll bet they just need a few slices of quince . . .

The Spuds at the door were somewhat bemused.
They could see that the boy was a little confused.
After all, he just stood there, bewildered and mute.
Then he brought them a plateful of yellowish fruit.

"No," said the Spuds. "Though this fruit is quite good,
we fear that, perhaps, you have misunderstood.
We're not here for pears, pineapples, or quince.
What we want is just you—to be our new *prince*."

Puggly still stood there, PALER than death.
He BLINKED. Then he nodded. Then he took a

DEEP BREATH.

"PRINCE PUGGLY," he whispered. "It sounds rather nice.

PRiNCE PUGGLY!"

he bellowed.

"Oh, it's worth saying twice."

"But wait," he reflected, and turned to the throng.
"Would you mind if I brought my great-granny along?"

Puggly, you see, did not live alone.
Out there on the moors, he was not on his own.
Inside the shack, there was someone else there,
someone quite old, with the palest of hair.

Someone *trembling* and stooped, with skin like a PRUNE,
or perhaps like a withered,
                         deflated
                              balloon,
with just a FEW TEETH, and hollowed-out cheeks,
and eyeballs so foggy they looked like antiques.

It was Puggly's great-granny! She lived in the back
of that muddy, that moldy, that tumbledown shack.
"Puggly," she said, her voice crackling but clear.
"Who are these people, and why are they here?"

Puggly explained, with a *quake* in his voice,
he'd been given a rather magnificent choice:
The Spudlian people had come to demand
that Puggly himself become Prince of the Land!

"Sounds fishy to me," his granny replied,
but she turned to the crowd with a measure of pride.
"My Puggly," she mused, "with a crown on his head!
I shall add it, right now, to my memoirs," she said.

You see, Puggly's granny had written for years,
recording her thoughts, her HOPES and her FEARS,
her PASSIONS, her *TRIUMPHS*, her
STRUGGLES and STRIFE.
Every occurrence from the whole of her life!

After all, she was old. What else could she do?
(You might want to write down your memories too.)

And by old, I mean *ancient*. She was on her last legs.
If she were a drink, she'd be down to the dregs.
If she were a car, she'd be covered in rust.
She was close, I'm afraid, to BITING THE DUST.

"Puggly? Go on then," she said with a sigh.
"I'll stay here and write. Or rather . . . I'll try.
I'll finish my memoir, before my demise!
But I'll miss you," she murmured,
with tears in her eyes.

When the Spudlians saw how this crusty old crone
would be left in the shack, in the mud, all alone,
they felt pity for her, their hearts seemed to swell,
and some of them even got teary, as well.

"Now, wait," said the Spuds, "we can't leave you here.
We can't take your Puggly and just disappear.
If we took him away, you would only be blue,
so Granny O'Bungleton, you can come, too!"

They returned to their carriage and went for a ride
(having loaded the boy and his granny inside).
They went wheeling and spattering over the **mud**
to the innermost heart of the

KINGDOM

OF SPUD...

Chapter 3
please, Not My Proust!

ONE

kingdom over,
in the Kingdom
of Spiff,
on the glittering ridge of
that Spiffian cliff,
King Dandy von Fop, that snob of a man,
still pestered his daughter, the princess called Fran.

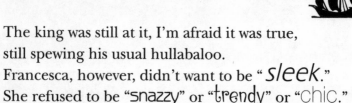

"Pajamas?" he muttered. **"With boats?!"** he exclaimed.
"How can you bear it? Aren't you ashamed?"

The king was still at it, I'm afraid it was true,
still spewing his usual hullabaloo.
Francesca, however, didn't want to be "*sleek*."
She refused to be "snazzy" or "trendy" or "chic."

She wasn't concerned with the latest of looks.
What concerned her, as always, were only her books.
"Oh, Daddy," she said, "you know that's not me.
You can bark all you want, but you've got the wrong tree.

"Don't try to tell me to wear something new.
I won't be convinced—not even by you.
So quit it, okay? I won't be induced.
I simply would rather be reading my Proust."

King Dandy, however, was set in his ways.
"Frannie," he grumbled, "your head's in a haze.
How is it you're always so far out of touch?
I mean, really, Francesca, this is too much.

"Our *Centenary Ball* is in less than a week!
People will think that I'm raising a freak.
They'll call you a dimwit, a fashion buffoon.
They'll say that you're **CRAZY**—as mad as a loon!

"But wait, it gets worse. And let me be clear.
Do you know who is coming? Do you know who'll be here?

Miss Ruby La Rue!

Of Ruby Boutique!

The ultimate maven of Spiffian chic!"
When he uttered the name, even Frannie grew STILL.
She shivered. She felt a disquieting chill.
Miss LaRue was a legend, the cream of the crop.
Her boutique was the kingdom's most popular shop.

Everywhere that you went, you would notice her face—

in commercials,

on billboards,
all
over

the

place,

simpering down with her powdery mug,
looking larger than life, and exceedingly smug.

"I don't care," said the princess. "Let her come if she wants,
with her fashion advice—or should I say *taunts?*
Because that's what they are. Let's be honest for once.
That woman's no more than a snobby old dunce!"

"*Sssshh!*" hissed the king. "What if somebody heard?
You can't really mean that. Please, don't be absurd."
He stomped with his foot (in its elegant shoe).
"We are talking, right now, about *Ruby LaRue!*

"In a *matter of days* she will come as our guest.
But you're wearing **pajamas!**
Oh, she won't be impressed.
So *please*—would you find something decent to wear?!
If Miss Ruby sees those, she'll have puppies, I swear!"

He was just getting ready to say something more
when a butler arrived to darken the door.
As perhaps you'd expect, he was dapperly dressed,
in a bow tie and tails and an elegant vest.

"Your highness, a message," the butler intoned.
He didn't quite speak, but rather, he *droned.*

With him, he carried a delicate tray.
It was silver, upon which an envelope lay.

"What's this?" asked King Dandy.
"Where is it from?
Tell me: Who sent it? From whence has it come?
Perhaps more importantly, what are these dots?"
(It was true: The paper was speckled with spots.)

Leaning over the tray to examine it close,
King Dandy exclaimed, "How insufferably gross!
This paper's besmirched with a sprinkling of crud!
"Can it be? Is this envelope spotted with—

M–M– MUD?!"

King Dandy, you see, was frightened of dirt.
If a smidgeon of DUST were to fall on his shirt
he would SCREAM like a child.
At times, he would faint.
If not, he would certainly voice a complaint.

"It's from Spud," said the butler, with a roll of his eyes,
and a look of disdain that he couldn't disguise.

"The Spuds?" said the king. "How unspeakably rank!
Of course we have only those dullards to thank.
With their kingdom of muck, their kingdom of sludge!
The whole of their land is one icky, brown SMUDGE!"

The butler agreed. He nodded his head.
"Your highness, you're right. They're awful," he said.
"But you've nothing to fear! Here is what I shall do:
I'll open this message and read it to you."

He picked up the paper as if it were cursed,
as if it were moldy, and ready to burst.
He unfolded the flap and extracted the note.
"Very well, then," he gulped. "It reads, and I quote:

'To our dearest fellow queens,
To our dearest fellow kings:
We are planning one of our
Extra-special gatherings.
Why? you ask. We're sad to say:
Because our king has run away.

When he vanished . . . Oh! Despair!
Yes, it's true: We thought it stunk.
WHY-OH-WHY?! That's what we thought.
(We assumed he must be drunk.)
Perhaps, we hoped, a brief sojourn?
Nope. The dope did not return.

But that's okay. We do not mind.
Who said we ever want him back?
In fact, we think that if he tried,
We would give him such a smack.
So yes, he's gone. Our king has fled.
But now we have a prince instead!

His name is "Puggly." He's a catch.
(He's nothing like that other guy.)
So come and meet him, here in Spud!

Oh, but hurry. Here is why:
His coronation happens soon.
In fact, it's right this afternoon!'"

When the butler had finished, he turned up his nose.
"It's *atrocious*," he muttered, "as poetry goes.
It started out bad, went straight on to worse.
A dismal example of doggerel verse!"

"You're right," said the king, "I quite see your point.
The rhythm, the rhyme—it's all out of joint.

But it came from the Spuds, and as everyone knows,
their poems are nearly as bad as their clothes.

"Yet sadly," he muttered, while wringing his hands,
"it's the law that the leader of each of the lands
must attend a new crowning . . . and so I shall go.
But those *Spuds*! They make me so *queasy*, you know?"

Indeed, he was green. He looked suddenly SICK.
His pallor went pasty. His forehead was *slick*.
He bent at the waist, his hands on his knees,
so the butler came over to put him at ease.

"There, there," said the servant. "I'm sure you'll be fine.
But those Spuds! I agree, they're no better than swine.
That clothing they wear? Oh, it's *all* out of **WhACK!**
Now here, let me help you by rubbing your back."

But the butler's massage wasn't very much help.
The king made a pitiful, whimpering yelp,
and then, with his head hanging down to the south,
he puked, just a little bit, into his mouth.

Meanwhile, Francesca, to a certain degree,
was intrigued. She looked up inquisitively.

"PUGGLY..."

she said. She savored the word.
"It's like no other name that I've ever heard."

She turned to the butler, with a questioning glance.
"This Puggly," she asked. "Is he bookish, perchance?"

The butler just shrugged and, clearing his throat,
said, "All I know is what's here, in this note."

In response, Frannie nodded.
She was thinking, you see.
"I wonder," she said, "is this Puggly like me?
Perhaps he likes books in a similar way.
Perhaps I should go to his crowning today."

Her father, however, set his hands on his hips,
His expression was SOUR (he was pursing his lips).
"Francesca," he said, his demeanor *SEVERE*.
"Unless you change clothes, you're staying right here!"

"But Dad," Frannie said, "that just isn't fair!
I love my **pajamas!** What else would I wear?"

"Well," said the king, "how about something nice?
Something regal for once, if you want my advice.
Something that wasn't just sewn out of **scraps**.
Something befitting a *princess*, perhaps?"

"Oh, Daddy," said Frannie. "**Pajamas** are fine.
They're simple and **FLUFFY** and rather benign.

Besides, it's a fact that a person succeeds,
not by her clothing, but rather her deeds."

"*Deeds?*"

cried the king. "Oh, don't be so soft!
All deeds do is make you all sweaty," he scoffed.
"No-no, I would argue, or rather, *insist*
that fashion's the reason that people exist!"

Francesca said nothing. Her only reply
was to open her book, with a shrug and a sigh.
But the sound of the CRINKLE that came from the page,
made her snob of a father fly into a rage.

He glared at his daughter.

"FRANCESCA!"

he roared.

"I'm your father, the king! I will not be ignored!
To you, it may seem like I'm making a fuss,
but it's clear to me now—your problem is thus:

"Reading all of those books
has made you **INSANE!**
It has poisoned your spirit
and addled your brain!
You no longer see clothes
in their natural role,
when in fact they're the core
of the Spiffian soul!

"Instead you read stories of lurid appeal,
and featuring people who *aren't even real*!
From now on, however,
there'll be no more pretend.
Your reading, my dear,
HAS COME TO AN END!"

He ordered his butlers, his soldiers, his staff
to remove every book, on his kingship's behalf.
He decreed, in a voice that was solemn and slow,
"You
    must
        lock
            every
                book
                    in the
                        dungeons
                            below!"

Frannie watched as they cleared every shelf, every nook,
and proceeded to lock away every last book.
~~HER DICKENS,~~
~~HER BRONTË,~~
~~HER AUSTEN,~~
~~HER POE~~ . . .
As her father decreed, they all had to go.

Her poetry too—~~HER ROSSETTI! HER POUND!~~
They vanished! It seemed they would never be found.
The princess, of course, was profoundly distraught.
Please, not my Proust! He's my favorite, she thought.

But they took every volume—all seven, in fact.
So SHOCKED was the princess, she could hardly react.
Her eyes filled with tears and she started to pout
(she could not stop a sniffle from snuffling out).

When the king saw his daughter so clearly upset,
he felt, for a moment, a pang of regret.
"I'm sorry," he told her. "Try not to be mad.
It's merely my duty, as a Spiffian dad.

"There's no need to cry, as I imagined you would.
Believe me, Francesca, it's for your own good.
No more novels and poems and all of the rest.
For once, you'll stop reading. You'll get up . . .
and GET DRESSED!"

He turned to his butler, who was there to obey,
in his usual cringing, obsequious way.
"Go and fetch," said the king, "my galoshes and coat,
and a silk that might cover my mouth and my
throat.

"And be certain the fabric is deeply perfumed.
If I breathe in that Spudlian air, I'll be doomed.

So be sure to use lots. I'll need all of it since
I am headed for Spud . . . to meet the new prince."

Then King Dandy von Fop, with a *quivering* heart,
plugged his nose with his fingers and turned to depart.

Meanwhile, Francesca felt lower
                              than
                                 low.
She had nothing to read and nowhere to go.
"What an absolute bummer," she sobbed to herself.
"There's nothing but **SHADOWS** on every last shelf!"

Lying back on her pillows in utter despair,
her head in a haphazard halo of hair,
her eyes full of tears and her nose full of snot,
she found there was something her father forgot!

Under her pillow, one book had been missed:

A single old copy of

Oliver Twist...

CHAPTER 4
a Brand-New Career

n

the Kingdom of Spud,
preparations were set
for a function that no one would
ever forget!

Every inch of the palace was primped to the gills
with **banners** and *spangles* and FRINGES and
frills;
with a fresh coat of paint (**they had laid it on thick**),
in colors so BRIGHT, it would make you feel sick!

True to form, they employed every possible hue.
The bailey was yellow, the barbican blue,
the parapet purple, the turret maroon,
and everywhere polka-dots—

big

the

as

moon!

"Amazing!" said Puggly, at all that he saw
as he wandered the castle, in obvious awe.
He strolled with his granny, out for a roam,
around their palatial (and soon-to-be) home.

"It's terrific!" said Puggly. He was beaming with pride.
Did you check out that *spire?* The one that's outside?"

"Of course I did, silly," was his granny's reply.
"I can see you're excited, but I'd like to know: *Why?*
Do you know what's to come?
Do you know what's in store?
Have you ever tried running a kingdom before?"

"Oh, Gran," Puggly started, "how hard can it be?
You sit on a throne, you make a decree,
you ride in a carriage, you wave and you smile,
then you dole out some knighthoods once in a while.

"Not to mention THE PARTIES!
They have those by the ton!
With mu$ic and streamers! Oh, won't it be fun!
With tinsel, confetti, maybe even BALLOONS!
And *dancing*—to the latest, most popular tunes!"

Puggly, you see, thought PARTIES were great,
but *why* he believed this was up for debate.
Although he was positive parties were **FUN**,
he had never—*not ever*—been invited to one.

His granny replied with a roll of her eyes,
"My boy, you are in for a nasty surprise!"
She was just about ready to say something more,
when a butler arrived, to darken the door.

(Now, while Spiffian butlers were GRAY and demure,
a Spudlian butler was different, for sure.
His livery jingled with baubles and bells
hung from his blazing, fluorescent lapels.)

Yet in spite of his dress, so flashy and wild,
the butler's demeanor was mellow and mild.
On his face was a gentle, congenial grin.
"Your highness," he bowed, "it's time to begin."

He led them away, t h r o u g h the palace's halls,
to a room deep within the palace's walls.

They arrived at a chamber,
EXPANSIVE and **ROUND**:
the place where the prince would be finally crowned.

It was brimming with people. The chamber was **PACKED**.
It was *teeming* and *swarming*, as a matter of fact.
Despite this, as Puggly stepped into the room,
the air fell as silent and STILL as a tomb.

He was brought to the stage and then, all alone,
he was pushed ^up the steps . . . and onto the throne.
He sat there, surveying the gathering crowd.
He admired their clothing. So garish! So loud!

His Spudlian heart was beating with glee,
as he looked on his people affectionately.
Behind him, the curtain was parted in two,
revealing a person that everyone knew.

THE SHAMAN OF SPUD! In a cassock of suede,
his bell-bottoms **STUDDED** with rubies and jade.

"Dear ladies and dudes," the Shaman began,
"today of all days is the **GROOVIEST**, man!
Today we are gathered for a Spud we revere.
That dude is the **P-MAN**, and he's sittin' right here."

He moved behind Puggly, to the rear of the throne,
and stood very **STILL**, like a figure in stone.

"On this noggin," he said, "on this coconut dome,
the Spudlian crown shall be makin' a home.
But before we do that, we must chill, we must wait.
Because first . . . I must bless the imperial pate!"

With both of his hands, with meticulous care,
he caressed Puggly's head and he fondled his hair.

Then he started to chant and started to sway
and put on a rather amusing display.
He shut both his eyes, *slipping into a trance*,
and boogied his way through the grooviest dance.

To Puggly, it all seemed a little BIZARRE.
He looked to his granny, who watched from afar.

She was squinting her eyes, a frown on her lips,
her hands pressing tight to her rickety hips.

"GROOOOOV-A-DELIC!" cried the
Shaman, his blessing complete.
He was panting by now. He was weak on his feet.
His exertions had left him all sweaty and red.
"Okay . . . we can start . . . with the crowning," he said.

He moseyed away, with his swaggering lope
to the edge of the stage, where he loosened a *rope*.
He unraveled the braiding, and upward it went,
going hand over hand, in a somber ascent.

In the dark of the ceiling, quite far out of reach,
a pulley was turning, with a creak and a screech.
The audience CRINGED at the SQUEAL of the gears,
for they hadn't been oiled in a great many years.

"Now," said the Shaman, "the moment is here,
for the P-MAN to kick off a brand-new career!
So here comes the crown, like a bird or a plane,
to circle around that incredible brain!"

Everyone saw it, as the braiding came down.
The end had been tied to the Spudlian crown.
It slowly emerged from the shadows above
like

an

angel,

a spirit!

Like a

heavenly

dove!

(No, wait. That's not true. It wasn't like that.
It was more like the world's most ridiculous hat.)

Puggly could see, though the lighting was dim,
there were quivering tassels that hung from the brim.
It was **MASSIVE**, as well, with buckles and straps.
A bit like a golden sombrero, perhaps . . .

Puggly felt, for a moment, a *tremor* of dread.
It was just as the crown settled down on his head.
He had feared that the thing would be grueling to wear,

air.

than

lighter

and

but in fact it was comfy,

It wasn't too l o o s e ; it wasn't too tight.
The fit on his forehead was perfectly right.
He buckled the buckles up, under his chin,
and rose from the throne, with his princeliest grin.

All at once, there were cheers. The band played a song,
with everyone happily clapping along.

Puggly thought: *Well! It's time for some fun!*
My reign as the Spudlian Prince has begun!

He looked to the Shaman, a little perplexed.
"Now what?" he whispered. "What happens next?"

"Next," said the Shaman, "is when you get to meet
other kings! Other queens!
Aw, it's gonna be **SWEET!**
They come from all over to give their congrats.
They'll be shakin' your hand!
They'll be tippin' their hats!"

He turned to the butler, who organized things.
"Send them in," he commanded.
"The queens and the kings!"

But the butler did nothing.
He looked sheepish and meek,
and he lowered his voice as he started to speak.
"There's a problem," he murmured. "It's kind of a shame.
Though I sent out the invites . . . almost nobody came."
"Oh . . . " Puggly sighed, upon hearing this news.
(He felt that his ego had suffered a bruise.)

Where are they? he wondered. From the **Kingdom of** *sleek*?
From the **Kingdom of** *Swish* and the **Kingdom of** chic?
They must think that we Spuds are completely uncool,
and since I am their prince, they must think me a *fool*.

"Wait," Puggly said, to the butler b
e
l
o
w.
"'*Almost*,' you said, and so I'd like to know:
Who was it that came?
There couldn't be n0ne.
'*Almost nobody came*'
means there had to be 1."

"One," said the butler. He let out a *s i g h*.
"This one . . . he's a rather unusual guy.
He claims he's the king from the kingdom next door,
and he says we should know him, that we've seen
him before.

But I can't really say if that is the case,
on account of the scarf he has tied round his face."

"A scarf?" Puggly asked. "Is that really true?
Only bandits wear masks. What a strange thing to do."

"Did you call me a bandit?!" cried a man at the back.
"How dare you cast forth such a savage attack!
I have come here today, to the 'kingdom' of Spud
with only the noblest and bluest of blood!"

The crowd opened up, so no one could miss
the stranger who suddenly said all of this.
They turned to the back and all of them saw
a man with a silk scarf over his jaw.

It covered his chin, his mouth, and his nose,
and perfectly matched with the rest of his clothes.

Oh! What an outfit! It was so very nice.
The colors were muted, the stitching precise.
From the cuffs to the cape to the velvety vest,
this stranger was rather stupendously dressed.

Yet a part of his outfit wasn't quite so urbane.
To be honest, it made him look rather inane.

I refer to his boots. They were buckled and laced
right the way up to the gentleman's waist!

"Your boots," Puggly said. "What's the story with those?
They don't seem to go with the rest of your clothes."

"I know!" cried the stranger,
stomping one giant boot.
"These galoshes have ruined the whole of my suit!
They're UGLY,
they're DRAB,
they dig into my gut,
and you have no idea how they chafe in the butt!

But I'm King of SPIFF, and this here is SPUD!
Perhaps you have noticed: IT'S COVERED IN MUD!"
As he said this, he shuddered, with a quivering voice.
"It ought to be clear, you have left me no choice!"

"King Dandy?" asked Puggly.
                              "I would never have guessed,
well, not by the way that you're currently dressed.
But thank you for coming, though you have to admit,
you do seem like a bandit. I mean, just a bit."

"YOU CAD!" spat the king,
through his delicate cloth.
It bounced off his mouth, like a fluttering moth.
"You did it again! I thought **once** would suffice,
but now I can see you've insulted me—twice!

"But coming from you, well—*HA!*—that's a laugh!
A donkey's more stylish than you, by a $1/2$!
Honestly, sir, I don't mean to be cruel,
but you dress like a slow-witted, nearsighted mule.
And you call that a crown? Outrageous!" he said.
"That looks like a *wagon-wheel* stuck on your head!"

The Spudlian people were shocked and amazed.
This Spiffian king—he surely was crazed!
Every face in the room was wearing a frown. :(
How dare he come here and disparage the crown?

In the heat of their rage, they sang out at once:

"King Dandy von Fop,
you insufferable dunce!

Our prince may dress oddly,
but none of us mind.
We know that this boy
is unselfish and kind!
He's our leader! Our chief!
And we don't give a fig
if there's too many curls
in his powdery wig!"

"**We like it,**" they cried, "if he looks like a kook!
We like that his shoes are the color of puke!
We like that his powdery wig is a mess!
We like that his cape is devoid of finesse!
We like that his breeches sag down in the butt!
If you think that's unstylish, then we say:
SO WHAT?!"

King Dandy fell silent, but his face had turned red.
"I can tell when I'm no longer wanted," he said.
For a moment, he *trembled*. Then he started to pout,
the cloth on his face puffing in, p u f f i n g   o u t.

"I'M GOING HOME!" he exclaimed,
with a sniff.

"I'll be glad to get back to my Kingdom of Spiff!"
He turned on his heel and he strode for the door,
his boots going squelchitty-squish on the floor.

The Shaman came over, saying, "Take it from me.
That Spiffian **DUDE?** He's out of his tree.
Completely neurotic, you see what I mean?
He's gotta **CHILL OUT**, lay off the caffeine."

"Uh, sure," Puggly said, with a nod and a smile.
His attention, however, had turned to the aisle.

He was searching for someone in the very back row.
Hadn't she been there, just a moment ago?
But although he looked *hither*

and

thither and yon,

he just couldn't find her. His granny was gone...

CHAPTER 5
the Nincomest Poop

A couple

days later, Prince Puggly awoke,
and threw on his noblest, most
beautiful cloak.
(Of course, I mean "beauty" in the Spudlian mode:
It had spots like a leopard, and it *actually* **GLOWED.**)

He had not seen his granny since the day he was
crowned.

This was mostly because he was never around.
After all, being prince kept him busy, you see.
There were people to meet and places to be.

His freest of time was the start of the day.
After breakfast was served
(on a **P O L K A - D O T** tray),
he then would go down

to

the

Library

Hall,

where bookcases *towered incredibly tall.*

Every shelf was replete with volumes galore.
There were even a few that were *piled on the floor.*

It was here that Prince Puggly had planted his throne.
And so, every morning, he went on his own
to pick up a book from a DUSTY OLD SHELF.
He'd meander its pages and read to himself.

the rise,
on
This particular morning, with the sun
Prince Puggly awoke to a pleasant surprise.
He was startled to see that a letter had come,
and was even more shocked to see who it was from.

"FROM SPIFF?" he exclaimed, as he looked at the stamp,
inspecting the envelope under a lamp.
"Their king, it would seem, thinks I look like a *fool*.
He compared how I dress to a dim-witted mule.

"And yes, while it's true that I'm new on the job,
it was clear that the man is a bit of a SNOB.
So why would King Dandy be writing to me,
after mocking my clothes so vociferously?"

He tore at the envelope, opened it wide,
and gasped when he saw what was waiting inside.

"Am I dreaming?" he wondered. "I can't be awake.
Can it really be true? Have they made a mistake?"

He held up the paper to examine the seal.
"No!" he exclaimed. "It appears to be real!
It's straight from the Spiffian powers that be.
An invite—to a PARTY—and it's written to me!"

Yes, my good reader, Prince Puggly was proud.
He held up his invite and read it aloud:

> *To Puggly, His Highness, the Prince of the Spuds:*
> *It's time to dress up in your gussiest duds!*
> *Spruce up your shoes and give them a shine.*
> *Be certain to wear something rather divine!*
>
> *Then come to the palace this Saturday night!*
> *Come for an evening of stylish delight,*
> *one that is sure to enchant and enthrall*
> *at the Spiffian People's Centenary Ball!*

When Puggly had finished, he felt a bit tense.
In Spiff, he surmised, they would spare no expense.
This PARTY of theirs would be one of a kind.

He could see it all now, in the eye of his mind.

Every inch of the Spiffian Palace would **GLOW**.
The turrets—all twelve—would be lit from below.
The guests will alight from their buggies and cars,
bedizened with JEWELS like the brightest
of stars!

They'll be throwing confetti
and B L O W I N G kazoos,
(with everyone wearing the fanciest shoes)!
Then Spiffian trumpets will trumpet a tune,
and play through the **NIGHT** by the LIGHT of the
MOON!

As he thought of the party, he started to fret.
His palms went all drippy with dribbles of sweat.
He was nervous, you see, from his cape to his core.
He had never once been to a party before.

And this was a *Spiffian* PARTY, no less!
The thought put the prince in a state of distress.
Every monarch alive would surely be there.
How would he face them? What would he wear?!

He looked down at himself, at his cape and his shirt,
their colors so brilliant, they actually hurt.
He examined his socks. They were two different types,
one ⓅⓄⓁⓀⒶ-ⒹⓄⓉ spots
and the other one STRIPES.

He thought of King Dandy, so perfect, so prim,
and dressed so dramatically different from him.
Despite the king's boots, with their squelchitty-squish,
the rest of his clothing was terribly swish.
It all went together, and everything fit.
He had looked pretty good, Puggly had to admit . . .

"What's the point?" the prince sighed.
"My clothes are absurd!
I can't face them like this. I look like a nerd.
My sleeves are too plaid, my trousers too short!
I've got all of the style of a festering wart!"

At last, he collapsed in the pit of his throne.

He felt hapless and hopeless . . . and very   alone.

(Except that he wasn't.)

There was someone else there.
It was someone quite old,
with the PALEST of hair;
someone with CRINKLED and wrinkled-up cheeks;
with eyeballs so foggy they might be antiques.

In an alcove, way off, in the back of the room,
his granny sat watching, concealed in a gloom.
She sagged like a willow tree over her desk,
with a posture so bent, it was rather grotesque.

The room that she sat in was dreary and dank.
On the desk, she had books, but the pages were blank.
That's because in her hand she was holding a quill.
She was writing, you see. She had pages to fill.

And fill them she did! Why, she wrote in a rage,
filling page after page after page after page!
She was writing her memoirs, just as she said.
She had vowed not to stop 'til the day she was dead.

"Boy?" said his granny. "Come closer, you hear?
I've something to say to that hole in your ear."

The crackling old voice gave Puggly a scare.
He'd had no idea that his granny was there.
"Who said that?" he whispered. He hardly could speak.
He uttered the words in a pitiful SQUEAK.

"It's me!" said the voice. "It's your granny, you nut,
and it sounds like you might need a kick in the butt!"
His great-granny trembled and waggled her fist.
"If it wasn't for me, then you wouldn't exist!"

In response to this rather emphatic remark,
Puggly stepped into the SHADOWY DARK.
"All right, then," he muttered in a sorrowful way.
"Here's my ear. What was it you wanted to say?"

"YOU'RE A FOOL!"
cried his granny, from her elderly stoop.
"YOU'RE A LUNKHEAD, MY BOY! YOU'RE THE NINCOMEST POOP!"
She picked up a notebook from under her rump,
and gave the boy's head a grandmotherly *THUMP*.

"Owww!" moaned the prince.
"Hey, what did I do?
How would you feel if I did that to you?"

"Hush," said his granny. "You deserved it, you see.
Now be a good princey and listen to me.
Those clothes you have on? They're not really so bad.
So what if they're printed with paisley and plaid?

"That's not who you are. It is merely décor.
Just rags on your back! That's all, nothing more.
Down deep
            in your
                    heart, you know who you are.
You're a Spudlian prince! And to me, you're a star.

"You are PUGGLY O'BUNGLETON!
            Prince of the Land!
You stand for the kingdom, do you understand?
So go to this PARTY! Who cares what they think!
If they say you're unstylish, you tell 'em:

THEY STINK!"

CHAPTER 6
a Simple Hello

On Saturday
night, at the palace of Spiff,
the scene on the crest of that
glittering cliff
was as Puggly imagined: all lit
                                    from below,
with the turrets like twelve giant candles, **AGLOW**.

From a distance, the palace was shining AND STILL,
like a sentinel, quietly waiting until
the first of the guests would begin to arrive,
as their horses and carriages came up the drive.

If you went closer, there was action and sound.
Servants and butlers, who bounded around
to the delicate **CLINKING** of saucers and forks
and the fizzle and popping of bottles and corks.

At last, the final arrangements were made:
Every elegant table was daintily laid.
The moat had been skimmed.
The lawn had been raked.
The fancy hors d'oeuvres were all perfectly baked.

With one final cl-*ip*, the hedges were pruned.
King Dandy was pleased. (He practically swooned!)

"I'm a genius!" he squealed, with a clap of his hands.
"It's the prettiest palace in all of the lands!
It's a towering triumph of stylish design!
But now, what to do with that daughter of mine?"

Indeed, the one thing that marred the décor,
were the princess's pillows, still

piled
on the
floor.

They were smack in the
middle
of *Frolicsome Hall!*,

on top (as I'm sure you recall).
with Frannie

For the king of the SPIFFS, the problem was thus:
If he asked her to move, she would kick up a fuss.
How was it, he wondered, she even was there?
On top of those pillows, way up in the air?

What was she doing? Wasn't she bored?
He had locked up the books she so dearly adored.
They were
deep
in his dungeon,
where they'd never be found.
So why was his daughter still lounging around?

"Francesca, my precious. My sweetie," he said.
"Shouldn't those pillows belong on a bed?
They really are such an embarrassing sight,
And you know very well,

it's our KINGDOM'S BIG NIGHT!"

"Indeed," she replied. "But I think that I'll stay.
I like it up here. It's comfy, okay?"

"Now, wait," said the king. "You must understand:
We start in five minutes! The time is at hand!
Francesca von Fop, you listen to me:
Get
   down
      from
         those pillows— IMMEDIATELY!"

For a moment, Francesca ignored the command.
She was focused, instead, on the thing in her hand . . .
At last, she said, "Sorry, were you speaking to me?
I was rather engrossed in my Dickens, you see."

As she said it, she knew she had made a mistake,
the worst kind of flub she could possibly make.
She had kept the book secret—at least until now.
It was something her father would never allow.
"Dickens?!" he cried.

"And you're 'rather engrossed'?
You say it so brightly, it sounds like a boast!
If there's Dickens up there—*and there'd better not be*—
I demand, as the king, that you show it to me!"

"Uhh ... *no*," said Francesca, with innocent eyes.
She batted her lashes in apparent surprise.
"Dickens? Oh, Daddy! That's not what I said.
What I said was, uh ... *chickens*! I said chickens,
instead."

The king was befuddled, rubbing his chin.
He hadn't the foggiest where to begin.
"Chickens?" he asked. "That doesn't make sense.
Are you having a joke at your father's expense?"

"Of course not," said Frannie. "You merely misheard.
Just now? I said 'chickens.' Yes, that was the word.
But don't worry. It's common,
happens all of the time.
Because Dickens and chickens—well,
see how they rhyme?"
"So it seems," said the king. "But is that really true?
You have *chickens* up there on those pillows with you?

If that's truly the case, I don't think it's right.
I assure you, those chickens aren't invited tonight!

They're *impossible* creatures! They squawk and they flap!
Do you *really* have chickens up there in your lap?"
He narrowed his eyes. "If so . . . let me see.
And why aren't they clucking conspicuously?"

Francesca turned PALE. She was caught in a lie.
"Just a second . . . I-I'll prove it," was her stammered
reply.

She folded a pillow up under her arm,
so it *slightly* resembled a bird on a farm.
But pillows and chickens are *not* the same thing,
and the effort fell short of convincing the king.

Down below, her father was shaking his head.
"Do you take me for some sort of ninny?" he said.
"That's not a chicken. It's a pillow, you brat!
Did you honestly think you could fool me with that?

"Well, you didn't," he said, with a withering look.
"So I'll have to assume that you're hiding a *book*,

and since you won't lock it away on a shelf,
I shall come up there now—and get it myself!"

He spit on his palms.
He glowered.
He frowned.

Then he started to climb up the pillowy mound.

Of course,

as he did,
it started to sway,
in a floppy
and rather
precarious way.

"Wait!" cried the princess. "You shouldn't! You can't!"
She could see they were teetering into a slant.

"Daddy! You're tempting the both of our fates!
This heap won't support the both of our weights!"

But the king kept on climbing, refusing to stop.

He scrambled and clambered, intent on the top.

Yet the whole of the heap was leaning, of course,
in defiance of every Newtonian force.

Although it was bending, it didn't collapse,
as if it was made out of rubber, perhaps.
But one thing was certain: It was no longer straight,
beset by the king's magisterial weight.

"Stop!" cried the princess. "We're going to fall!
We'll go splattering all over *Frolicsome Hall!*"

But King Dandy kept climbing, ignoring her pleas.
He climbed with his feet, his fingers, his knees.

Until, at long last, he had scaled to the peak,
which somehow supported his kingly physique.

Hanging and flailing, like a fish on a hook,
he pointed and shouted:
"I KNEW IT! A BOOK!"

But sadly the king was too eager, too proud,
(which is probably why he was shouting so loud).
So as he yelled *"BOOK!"*—at that moment in time,
the sound of the word put an end to his climb.

He heard from below him . . . the tearing of threads!
The fizzle of fabric being ripped into shreds!
The s p l i t t i n g of seams! The *unravel of yarn!*
All that King Dandy could say was:

"Oh, darn."

Then father and daughter, with cushions and all,
fell from the rafters of Frolicsome Hall.

The landing they landed with could have been rough,
if not for the mountain of stuffing and **FLUFF**.

What once was a mountain was a mountain no more.

Its pillows had

ruptured all over the floor.

thankfully spilling their cottony guts,
as the king and his daughter came down on their butts.

Francesca went *thump*, with an almighty "OOF!"
She looked at her father and thought, *What a goof.*
"Daddy," she muttered. "I think I can say,
you have quite absolutely ruined my day!"

She was just getting ready to say something more,
when a stranger appeared, to darken the door . . .

This person strode in with a purposeful stride.
He held up his nose as he sauntered inside.
Musicians were with him. They blew o u t a tune.
The first on a trumpet; the other, bassoon.

When the fanfare subsided, the man took a bow.
"Fear not!" he announced. "I am here with you now!
You may clap if you like. You are welcome to cheer.
The superlative prince-among-princes is here!"

"Big whoop," said Francesca, still slumped on the floor.
"After all, it's not like I've met you before.
In fact, I am hardly aware you exist.
Now let me get back to my *Oliver Twist*."

The gentleman guest was entirely shocked.
"**You mock me!**" he roared.
"**I should never be mocked!**
If you knew who I was, you would zip up that lip!
For I am Prince Hep of the Kingdom of **HIP!**"

To prove it, the prince did a bit of a jig,
while flipping and fluffing his feathery wig.
He showed off his robes—every fold, every pleat,
from his cuffs, to his cloak, to the shoes on his feet.

"I'm exquisite!" he cried. "And I'm sure you can see.
I am always attired *magnificently*!
Why, even my skivvies, under my clothes
are *rousingly* chic, as everyone knows!"

"**Blegh**," Frannie said. "I do *not* need to know.
All you needed to say was a simple hello."

"'Hello?'" asked the prince. "Dear girl, are you mad?
That just wouldn't do! And I hasten to add,
you need trumpets and *music* on a night like tonight.
A simple 'hello'? No, that wouldn't be right.

An evening like this, I would humbly suggest,
is for making an entrance, while looking your best!"
He completed this thought with a bit of a *twirl*.
He spread out his arms and went for a *whirl*.

"Take *me* for example. So *REFINED!* So precise!
One simple 'hello' would never suffice.
My greatcoat, my epaulets, my pantaloons, too.
All the latest designs from *Miss Ruby LaRue!*"

Francesca replied, "Miss Ruby La . . . *who*?"
when in actual fact, she already knew.
But this Prince of the **HIP** seemed like such a big dolt,
she couldn't help wanting to give him a jolt.

"What?!" the prince yawped. He was utterly shocked.
He stood there
                and swayed,
          like his
                world had
          been rocked.

"*Miss Ruby*," he said. "She's the finest around!
The woman's revered. Respected! *Renowned!*

"Surely, you've heard of the Ruby Boutique!
The vanguard of style! The temple of chic!
All of my clothes, every marvelous thread,
Miss Ruby designs . . . *just for me*," the prince said.

"Ho hum," Frannie yawned.
"Do you think I'm impressed?
There's more to a person than how they are dressed."

WHEN SHE SAID THIS, IT SEEMED LIKE THE UNIVERSE
STOPPED.
IT FELT LIKE THE TEMPERATURE SUDDENLY DROPPED.
THE WHOLE OF THE PALACE WAS SUDDENLY HUSHED.
PRINCE HEP WENT ALL RED (HE WAS THOROUGHLY
FLUSHED).

"Disgraceful! Preposterous! *Outrageous!*" he spat.
"How dare you say something so silly as that?!
There is nothing more grand than the clothes on
your back!
But grandness—quite clearly—is something you lack!

"You've no sense of fashion! Why, look at you there!
That looks like an outfit a monkey would wear!

Those **Pajamas!** Those slippers! You look like a wench!
Do you wear that all day? Just imagine the **STENCH!**"

"Now wait," said the king, who of course was nearby.
"As the princess's father, I cannot deny
that my daughter's pajamas are . . . eccentric at best.
And frankly, let's face it, she's a bit underdressed.

"But I cannot abide you disparaging her.
It's rude and uncouth. I won't stand for it, sir!
She may be a *schlub*, and a book-lover, too,
but you can't call her *smelly*! That just isn't true."

The prince turned his face to Francesca, and then:
He slowly looked back at King Dandy again.

"You're one to talk," said Prince Hep, with a sneer.
"Like father, like daughter—that much is clear.
Have you looked at yourself? Your robes are in rags.
They look more like shredded-up grocery bags!"

Slowly, King Dandy looked down at his clothes.
The moment he saw them, he suddenly **FROZE**.

It was true: They were torn. Prince Hep was correct.
And not merely ripped. His robes had been

WRECKED.

His trousers, his cape, his silken chemise,
they were torn into shreds.
They were grated, like cheese.
Because all his clothing had fitted so well,
there was nearly no room for the fabric to swell.

When King Dandy had climbed up those pillows before
and then, when he tumbled

          back down

             to the floor,
every seam on his body, every single last one,

had burst

(or at least had come partly undone).

So his clothes hung in tatters, ragged and THIN.
He looked like a lizard, half-moulting its skin.

It was clear from the TERRIFIED look on his face,
for the very first time, he was feeling ... *disgrace.*
He had lost all his confidence, lost all his pomp.
He resembled a creature dredged up from a swamp.

He
took
a step
backward,
in fear, in retreat
(not seeing the pillows piled up at his feet).
So of course, when he hit them,
he stumbled and *trip*ped.
He went tottering backward.
He *skittered* and skip*ped.*

He kicked up the stuffing that covered the floor,
and went floundering through it—right out the door!

Meanwhile, Prince Hep was wearing a smile,
but it wasn't a pleasant one (not by a mile).
It was more of an arrogant, cynical smirk,
confirming the prince was a bit of a jerk.

In fact, he was worse than a jerk or a goof,
and when he spoke next, he offered the proof.

"Pajamas," he laughed.
"That's the best you can do?
No wonder your father's embarrassed with you.
You're not any princess, you're more of a frump.
The whole of that outfit belongs in a dump!"

Hearing Prince Hep, as he vented his spleen,
Francesca felt awful, not fit to be seen.
She felt like a bug, or a bump on a log.
She felt like a wart on the back of a frog.

She thought to herself, *What can I do?*
What if he's right? What if it's true?
Could that happen for real? Could it actually be?
Could my father, the king, be *embarrassed* with me?!

"Maybe . . . you're right," she said, with a sigh.
Then she covered her face, and she started to cry.
Her Dickens—*her book!*—slipped out of her lap,
and fell to the floor with an audible *slap*.

Frannie, by now, was so deeply despaired,
she left it and r a n. She no longer cared.
She r a n past the king, who was sprawled in a heap,
lying there, groggy, and mostly asleep.

Yet just at that moment, King Dandy awoke
(when his daughter ran over the shreds of his cloak).

"Francesca!"

he hollered, but he was too late.

His daughter, already, had r u n

for the gate . . .

CHAPTER 7
irrefutable Facts

OUT

on the road to the palace of Spiff, where it skirted the edge of its glittering cliff, a carriage approached. It trundled along, but something about it was just a bit ... wrong.

Now, a *Spiffian* carriage was a beautiful thing. Its gilding and velvet were fit for a king!

It was music in motion, refinement on wheels,
more posh than the ritziest automobiles!

Conversely, the carriage approaching that night
was a pitiful, rather precarious sight.

Who would ride in a carriage so rusty and old?
So lacking in style (and with so little gold)?
Instead, it was painted with SQUIGGLES
and **blobs**,
with higglety-pigglety *swishes* and swabs.

Who would come in a carriage so undignified?
With a cabin like that—with horns on the side?!
(That's right, it had horns! They stuck in the air,
like the helmet a lopsided Viking would wear!

Who would ride in a clunker that
bumped on the ground,
on wheels that were EGG-SHAPED, rather than round?
With lights that were flashing electrical pink?!
Who was inside?

(Well, who do you think?)

PRINCE PUGGLY, of course. He was seated within,
quite nervous, with goose-pimples pricking his skin.

The driver quite suddenly pulled on the reins.
The horses reared up, with their shivering manes.
They ended their flop-footed clippity-clop,
as the carriage was brought to a juddering **STOP**.

"Regrets," said the driver, "but that wasn't my fault.
I never meant to pull up for so hasty a halt.
See, I was just sittin' here. Just driving, okay?
When this girl? She comes running, gets right in my way!"

"A girl?" Puggly asked. He sat up in his seat.
He peered out the window and into the street.
Indeed, there she was: a girl, r u n n i n g *past*.
She seemed rather troubled. She was r u n n i n g quite
f a s t .

"You're right," Puggly said, in utter surprise.

"If I'm not mistaken, she had *tears* in her eyes!
Perhaps," he called up to the carriage chauffeur,
"we ought to go see what was bothering her."

"Wish I could," said the driver, "I honestly do,
but just look behind us. That's some kinda queue!
This road is backed up to the Kingdom of Swish.
So what'll I do, pull a U-ey? *I wish!*"

Indeed, it was true. There was nowhere to go.
BEHIND
THEM
WERE
CARRIAGES,
ALL
IN
A
ROW.

The driver behind them was shaking his fist.
"You lazy, malingering laggards!" he hissed.
"Get that *monstrosity* out of the way!
Go on, then! Get moving! And I mean—TO-DAY!"

"All right," Puggly sighed, with a hand on his brow.
"That girl who we saw must be far away now."
He rapped on the roof and said, "Driver, drive on.
Whoever she was, she appears to be gone."

The driver complied. He was silent above,
the reins in the clutch of his leathery glove.
Puggly heard only the CLOP and the CLIP,
as the horses went cantering on with the trip.

He thought to himself, from his seat in the rear:
Why would some woman be fleeing from here?
And what was she wearing? **Pajamas**, I think,
while her feet were adorned with slippers of pink . . .

But his thoughts turned away from the girl, and her fate,
when the driver pulled up to the palace's gate.

With his carriage *ablaze* in the *Spiffian* light,
Prince Puggly was suddenly FROZEN in fright.
He felt timid and doubtful, incredibly shy.
He peeked from his window with only one eye.

A lump started growing at the back of his throat.
For here were the gardens, the turrets, the moat.
With one look at the palace, he said, "*Holy cow!*"
This was different from Spud; that was obvious now.

Every guest looked so cool! They seemed so at ease!
While Puggly felt nauseous, and weak in the knees.

It made him feel ... *different*. Unworthy and plain.
As bare and exposed as a worm in the rain.

"No," Puggly whispered. "I can't go in there."
They'll never accept me, he thought in despair.
"Driver?" he called. "Take me back where I'm from.
I'm out of my league. I should never have come."

"Now, wait," said the driver, "at least *try* to get out.
It's a PARTY! It's no time to sit here and pout.
I mean, sure—our kingdom's not stylish or rich.
Our clothes're peculiar and sometimes ... they ITCH.
But Puggly, your highness, with all due respect,
you might need to get that head of yours checked.

"Don't forget who you are. You're the one we all chose.

We chose *you*—Prince Puggly—*because* of your clothes!
So despite what you're thinkin', you belong here tonight.
You're a **PRINCE!** And besides…they invited you, right?"

Puggly sat and unfolded the invite once more.
He looked down at the Spudlian clothes that he wore.

He's right, Puggly thought, I belong here! *I do!*
From the tip of my crown to the sole of my shoe!
I've no need to worry; I've no need to wince.
My clothing, quite rightly, is fit for a prince!

So when

Puggly stepped out, he was preening and PROUD

(in spite of the shrieks from the gathering crowd).

"Who is *that*?!" they called out.

"What a fashion-less mess!

What a **boob!**

What a *schlub!*

Like, where's the finesse?

Look at those stockings!

One orange?

One green?

That's the worst sense of fashion that we've ever seen!"

"But the wig!" said a voice. "That wig is *the worst*! What is that, *a rat*?! The thing must be cursed!"

The woman who uttered these muttering words
had a fluttering voice, like the chirping of birds.
She wasn't quite old and she wasn't quite young.
She was staring, disgusted, and clucking her tongue.

But in spite of a face that was cranky and cross,

her clothes had a radiant, shimmering gloss,
The threads of her dress, every glimmering stitch,
were *stylish* and PERFECT and *regal* and rich.

Her skirt was in layers (this was very in-style),
while her wig was pinned up in a delicate pile.
Her hems had been daubed in the subtlest dye,
and her jewelry twinkled like stars in the sky.

When the crowd saw her coming, they parted and bowed
(they
    were
        stooping
            as low as
                their
                    bodies
                      allowed).
It was clear from her clothing, so carefully sewed:
She was hip! She was cool! She was sooooo à la mode!

Who was this woman? (I'll bet you know who.)
This person, of course, was

Miss Ruby LaRue!

The finest of fashion designers around!
She looked at Prince Puggly, however, and frowned.

"What a wig!" she cried out.
"What a man! What a mess!
What unstylish, unsightly, unseemly excess!"
She covered her mouth with the silk of her scarf.
"Oh, fetch me a bucket! I think I may barf!"

It seemed so, indeed. She heaved and she retched,
and as she requested, a bucket was fetched.
But there was no puke. She vomited not,
despite being given a vomiting pot.

(If she barfed, after all, she would look like a freak.
Spewing up lunch was *so* very last week.)

"That outfit!" she cried.
"It boggles the mind!
If I look any more,
I think I'll go blind!
Who *are* you?" she asked.
"You must tell us your name.
I need to know who would wear something so *lame*."

Hearing these insults, poor Puggly was flushed.
His spirits d
        e
        f
        l
        a
        t
        e
        d. His confidence CRUSHED.
A million misgivings were filling his brain,
but finding some courage, he tried to explain.

"I'm a p-prince," he insisted. "I-I'm new on the scene.
So sure, I might come off a little bit green,
but I'm in the right place. I don't mean to boast,
but they sent me an invite! It came in the post!"

"Give that to *me!*" snapped Ruby LaRue.
"Why would *anyone ever* have sent one to you?"
She grabbed the poor prince by the thin of his wrist,
and wrangled the invite from out of his fist.

"You realize," she sneered, "you can never be swish,
when you're wearing a tie that is shaped like a *fish!*

No-no, it is clear there has been a mistake.
You're a fraud, I'm afraid. This invite's a fake."

"No!" Puggly cried. "I had it all checked!
The address, the postage! It all was correct!"

"Perhaps," Ruby smiled. "Or so it would *seem*.
But you're clearly mistaken—and in the extreme!
But let us be certain. Let us *compare*.
Your invite . . . with mine. I think that is fair.

"And, oh, aren't we lucky! I have mine right here!"
She gently produced it from within her brassiere.
"Now we shall see: Who is wrong? Who is right?
Or to be more precise, who's the LIAR tonight?!"

She inspected the paper for a moment or two.
"Aha!" she cried out. "The liar is **YOU**!"

"It can't be!" was Puggly's insistent reply.
"I'm telling the truth! I never would lie!"

"But you are," Ruby muttered. "I knew all along.
This glue is too gummy. The folds are all wrong.

Just look," she showed Puggly. "Any halfwit could see:
This invite's been forged, *unequivocally*!

"The paper's TOO THIN. Just look how it droops!
And this curlicue here? Why, there's too many loops!
Moreover, it's sealed with inferior wax!
Good sir, are these not **IRREFUTABLE FACTS**?!"

"But my name," Puggly whispered. "On the envelope, see?
'PRINCE PUGGLY,' it says. That really is me."

He reached out and said, "Please, give it back."
Ruby, however, gave his hand a great *smack*,
and Puggly was forced to watch in dismay,
as she tore up his invite and threw it away.

The wind took the bits, with a WHOOSH
and a *whiff*,
and sent them all
fluttering
over the cliff.

"No!" Puggly whimpered. He threw his arms wide.
"Why did you do that? How could you?!" he cried.

"WHY?" asked one guest.
"What are you, an ape?!
It's because of those breeches!
Because of that cape!"

"That's right," said another,
"we all here concur:
It's because of that tie—and that cardigan, sir."

"On your knee," said another,
"there's a corduroy patch!
And your stockings, you boob!
They don't even match!"

"Those buttons!" cried everyone.
"They're wooden, you hear?!
WOOD?!! Hasn't been in since June of last year!
Not to mention your crown!
What an utter disgrace!
Let's be honest. It looks like a frisbee from space!

"Then there's your sleeves!
Just look at that cuff!
Boy! You'd be better off bare,
in the buff!
To sum up, that outfit isn't fit for a pig!
But mostly, you twit, it's BECAUSE
OF THAT WIG!"

Puggly said nothing. He swayed on his feet.
He felt useless, unwanted, quite obsolete.
He blinked, only once. Then he uttered a sigh.
"Oh…" he said slowly. "So now I know why."

Then he turned from the crowd and the palace of Spiff,
and though both his legs felt empty and stiff,
he stumbled away, looking ghostly and frail,
his eyes glazing over, his face going pale.

His driver awaited, by the drawbridge, out front.
He had heard how his prince had suffered the brunt
of so many taunts and so many jeers.
He saw that the eyes of his prince were in tears.

"C'mon," said the driver, "I think we should go.
That *Ruby's* a wacko. She's crazy, y'know?"

He opened the door of the carriage's cab,
but Puggly just stood there, dreary and **drab**,
as empty and PALE as the palace's wall.
He didn't climb into the carriage at all.

"No," he said softly. "Miss Ruby was right.
I'm simply not stylish enough for tonight.
I thought I liked parties and dancing and stuff,
but now I've decided . . . these parties are rough.

"They make you feel awful, but at least now I know,
what happens at parties, when you actually go.
Anyway, they were right. Just look how I dress.
If the clothes make the man . . . then I've made a mess."

He looked down at his feet. He closed both his eyes.
Then he took off his crown, with the deepest of sighs.
He handed it back to the driver and said,
"This crown, I believe, was too good for my head."

He followed these words with the tiniest smile.
"I think someone else should be prince for a while."
With that, poor old

Puggly

just wandered

away,

like a ship gone adrift,

or a dog gone astray . . .

CHAPTER 8
the Queen of the Slobs

etween
the two kingdoms
was nothing but trees.

They *blew* in the swish of the Spiffian BREEZE.
Maples and beeches and poplars and pines,
all of them dripping with creepers and VINES...

They made up a forest, forbidding and dense.
It sprawled on for miles (it was rather immense).
Right through the center, a river of blue
neatly divided the forest in two.

The banks of the river weren't quite so pristine,
not nearly so fresh, not nearly so clean.
This was near Spud, where the land was a swamp,
where you couldn't just stroll, you more had to tromp.

The ground was all clammy, as slimy as **SNOT**,
besotted with fungus and festering rot.
There was life there, of course, but it mostly was bugs.
There were **SPIDERS** and ants and especially
slugs.

Crossing over the river, in an elegant arc,
was a bridge made of stones; they were mossy and dark.
Down below,
underneath it,
where nobody went,
where the riverbank oozed
in its gooey descent,
was a *princess*.

(Yes, that one).

She was flopped on a log,
like a rag, or a sloth, or some miserable frog.

"Prince Hep!" she lamented. "I guess he was right.
I belong in a dump! I'm a **miserable** sight!
Even though he's a jerk and the prince of the snobs,
he was right about me—I'm the queen of the **slobs**!"

Quite clearly, the princess was down

                      in

                           the

                               dumps,
(amid fungus and mushrooms and moldy old stumps).
Yet insults alone were not nearly enough
to upset a princess so stubborn, so tough.

She had heard the same thing from her father for months:
In her flannel **pajamas**, she looked like a dunce.
But her father's derision was never so bad—
not from a loveable goof like her dad.

For in spite of his jibes, in spite of his digs,
in spite of his perfectly powdery wigs, **SHOUT**,
in spite of the way he would holler and **SHOUT**,

his LOVE for the princess was never in doubt.

Yet that's how she felt: doubtful, confused;
her spirit unsettled, her confidence bruised.
Is it true, she was thinking, what Prince Hep had claimed?
My father's embarrassed—or even ashamed?

of hair?

n
o
i
t
p
u
r

Ashamed of my slippers, my e
Ashamed of these silly **pajamas** I wear?
Could it be that my father, my very own dad,
would believe such a thing? Well, that makes me MAD!

"Fine, then!" she cried. "I shall never go back!
I shall live here alone, in a little grass shack.
Here in the woods, in the **SHADE OF THIS BRIDGE.**
I'll set up my home at the foot of this ridge.

I have water and shelter and all I could need!
The only thing missing is ... *something to read.*"

The moment she said it, she knew she was s

                                                    u

                                                        n

                                                            k.

Her head started spinning, as if she were ***drunk***.

"NO BOOKS!"
she bewailed, to the brambles and twigs.
"NO BOOKS!"
she bemoaned, to the sprouts and the sprigs.
"It's appalling! Atrocious! Abysmal! Absurd!
There's NOTHING to read!
Not even ONE WORD!"

Francesca was right. It was certainly true.
Without any books—well, what would she do?
Nothing, she thought. I'll do nothing at all.
My life will be dim as a hole in a wall.

But before she could tip into total despair,

The noise was the crunching of gravel and peat,
a meandering stagger, a stumble of feet.

Footsteps! Francesca was quick to surmise,
peering up at the bridge and shielding her eyes.
An oddly dressed boy, in a *l i n g e r i n g* lope,
                              slope.
                        of the
                    top
                  the
was plodding along at

He tramped and he trudged, as he came up the road.
When he got to the bridge, his wandering slowed.
He stopped in the middle. He leaned on the rail.
The whole of his person was weary and PALE.

"THE SPIFFS!" he spat out, in a **venomous** voice.
"I would send them all packing, if I had a choice!
Back at their palace, I was treated like **DIRT**!
To be treated so badly—well, that really hurt.

"They deflated my ego! They punctured my pride!

I felt TWO INCHES TALL! I felt *awful* inside!
It's *degrading*!" he grumbled. "*Demeaning*!" he hissed.
"I'm a prince!" he cried out, with a shake of his fist.

"So it would seem," Francesca agreed.
"Your manner and bearing are *regal*, indeed.
You say you're a prince? I believe that you are,
despite wearing clothes that are . . . rather BIZARRE."

A voice, Puggly thought, but coming from where?
Peering over the railing, he saw someone there.
A girl sat below him. On a stump. In the **mud**.
"Hello there," he said. "You must be from Spud!"

The girl shook her head. "Well, actually, no.
I'm a SPIFF," she called up from the gully below.
"I'm the *princess*, in fact, which is how I could tell,
that you, sir, up there, were royalty, as well."

"Funny," said Puggly, "you don't look like a SPIFF.
But if so, you'll forgive me for wondering if
you're about to berate me, to show me contempt,
to call me *'unstylish, unworthy, unkempt,'*
to heckle my clothing and spray me with scorn,

to *insult me*—so I'd wish that I'd never been born!
Well, don't waste your breath.
I've had enough for one day.
I've had all that a person can handle, okay?"

"No," said the princess. "I would never! *I can't!*
But I totally know why you went on a rant.
I grew up in that palace. It was *quite* the ordeal.
So believe it or not . . . I know how you feel."

They were silent a moment.
They STOOD there and stared,
regarding each other, until PUGGLY declared,
"I believe you. I do." He could see it was clear,
this girl down
            below him was being sincere.

"You know," he went on, "it's quite a relief,
finding someone to share in a bit of my grief.
It's nice to meet someone with whom you agree.
Those Spiffs? *No-no-no!* Not our cup of tea!
Now, I know I've not made your acquaintance as yet,
but you seem *so familiar.* Have you and I met?"
"I don't think so," said Fran.

"But I'm a bit out of touch.
It's why I like wearing pajamas so much."

"Pajamas!" cried Puggly. "I've seen them before.
It was *you* coming out through the palace's door!
You were r u n n i n g away. You were crying, I think.
Yes, I remember your slippers! They're pink."

Frannie looked down. She wiggled her toes.
"My father," she sighed. "He's all about *clothes*.
But I prefer books. It's just who I am.
And so I decided to go on the lam."

"On the lam?" Puggly asked. "But where will you go?
Living
    under
        a bridge
            won't
                be easy, you know."

"Where else can I live?" was Francesca's reply.
"All the rest are the same, all the kingdoms nearby.
There's the **Kingdom of** *sleek* and the **Kingdom of** chic.

In either, I wouldn't last more than a week!
The **Kingdom of Mod**? **Kingdom of FAD**?
I think we both know that they're equally bad.
Perhaps worst of all is the **Kingdom of HIP**.
I can tell you, *for sure*, I'll give that one a skip.

"The way that I see it, every kingdom's the same.
All following fashion, all playing the game.
So instead, I'll live here, in this leafy a
                                          b
                                          y
                                          s
                                          s.
There's no kingdom out there that's better than this."

"Wait," Puggly said. "There's a kingdom you missed,
one kingdom you didn't include on your list."
Francesca was puzzled on the stump where she sat.
"Oh?" she inquired. "What kingdom is that?"

"SPUD!" Puggly told her, a grin on his face.
"It's all covered with **mud**! It's a wonderful place!
You might think our clothing's a little bit strange,

but you're welcome to visit. You know, for a change."

"Sounds nice," Frannie said. "Well, *the mud* . . . maybe not.
But this **Kingdom of SPUD**, I could give it a shot.
It's certainly better than living outdoors.
Perhaps I could move to this kingdom of yours . . ."

Soon they were chatting like the oldest of chums,
laughing and chuckling and flapping their gums.
With so much in common, they made quite a pair,
and when speaking of SPIFF, they had plenty to share.

"I wish," Puggly said, after sharing his woes,
"they hadn't so harshly insulted my clothes.
I felt like an oaf, like a blundering dunce.
I wish I could teach them a lesson for once!"

"Maybe you can," Francesca replied.
She climbed up to Puggly, and stood by his side.
Cupping her mouth, with both of her hands,
she leaned to his ear, and whispered her plans.
Puggly's expression, at first, was intense.
The princess's words didn't seem to make sense.
But it soon became clear and he then understood:

The *princess's* plan ... it was rather quite good!

Chapter 9
nothing Else More

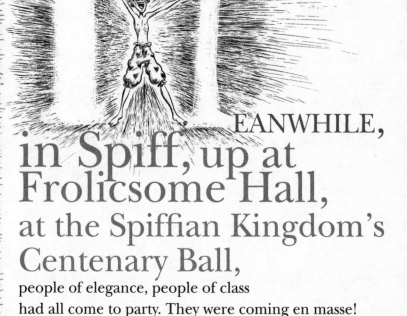

MEANWHILE,
in Spiff, up at
Frolicsome Hall,
at the Spiffian Kingdom's
Centenary Ball,
people of elegance, people of class
had all come to party. They were coming en masse!

From the **Kingdom of HIP**, the **Kingdom of** *sleek*,
the **Kingdom of** *Swish* and the **Kingdom of** chic,
from the **Kingdom of Mod** and the **Kingdom of** FAD,
every one of them posh, and impeccably clad.

The revelers rollicked and mingled and danced!
They chortled and chuckled!
They prattled and pranced!
Every face in the room was impossibly swank,
and of course they had only King Dandy to thank.

But where was he? they wondered. He ought to be here.
Would he leave them alone?
WOULD HE JUST DISAPPEAR?
Where was their gracious and jovial host?
It would seem he had vanished, as if like a GHOST!

(Except that he hadn't.)

King Dandy was there.
He was up in his chambers, slumped in a chair.
You see, my good reader, King Dandy was sad.
He might have been "king," but he'd flunked as a dad.

"I'm a fraud," he lamented. "A failure, a flop!
I'm a phony! A fool! I'm a *poop* of a pop!
I'm simply no good. My life is a sham!
The worst father ever—that's what I am!"

As you can see,
the king was upset.
He burned with remorse! He flambééd with regret!
(You can't blame him, of course. He was that sort of king.
Melodramatics were clearly his thing.)

"I'm sorry," he whimpered. "I have no excuse.
"My marbles were muddled! My screws had come loose!
Wait a minute! That's it! Now I know what it was!
I was sweating to death—under all of this FUZZ!"

What he meant was his wig. He yanked the thing off.
"It was ITCHY, as well," he said, with a scoff.

He tossed the insufferable thing on the floor.
"I won't be a slave to that wig anymore!"
He panted. He seethed. He was deeply appalled.
(He had also revealed he was thoroughly bald.)

At the party, meanwhile, the lute-players strummed;
the flute-players whistled; the drum-beaters drummed.
The palace's band had struck up a song,
with the revelers lumpishly waltzing along.

Although they were hip, they danced like buffoons.
It looked like a room full of woozy baboons!
They staggered and stumbled.
They *tumbled* and *trip*ped.
They f l o u n d e r e d and flummoxed
and fumbled and *flip*ped.

In the midst of this klutzy, incompetent zoo,
was the fashion designer, *Miss Ruby LaRue*.
She danced with Prince Hep,
from the **Kingdom of HIP**,
careening around like a rudderless ship.

At the end of the song, they let out a wheeze.
They were gasping for breath, their hands on their knees.
"I'm pooped," Ruby said, as she clung to Prince Hep.
"My legs are *kaput*! I can't take one more step."

As she voiced her fatigue, as she limped for a chair,
as she smoothed out her dress and fluffed up her hair,
as she moaned to Prince Hep,
"I CAN'T DANCE ANYMORE!"
it was then someone **rapped** on the palace's door.

The whole of the chamber WENT STILL AS A TOMB.
Every curious eye in the luminous room
regarded the door, then **widened** in shock,
as the stoical butler unbolted the lock.

Then, with a creak, the door opened wide,
and there was a girl. She was standing outside.
The guests were all SHOCKED!
They clutched at their throats.
This girl wore **pajamas** … printed with boats!

"Oh," said Prince Hep, "not you again. *Please*!
Your clothes give me hives. I think I may sneeze."

"Indeed," said Miss Ruby. "What's wrong with you, dear?
Are those *PJs* you're wearing?
Well, they don't belong here.
This PARTY'S for people
with *grace* and with *style.*
And you don't have either—not by a mile."

"Maybe I don't," Francesca replied.
"I'm not very *stylish*, that can't be denied.
I'm not very cool. I don't create 'buzz.'
But I brought with me someone who certainly does!"

She stepped to the side, and everyone FROZE.
A man stood behind her . . . in the strangest of clothes.

His cloak had been sewn out of festering leaves,
with FUNGUS for cuffs at the end of his sleeves.
His trousers were **mossy**. They were sewn out of peat,
and slithered with snails, from his hips to his feet.

His wig, made of TWIGS, was unruly indeed.
It fell over his face like a copious weed.
On top was a hat made of *very* soft fruit.
It was rotten, in fact. Quite smelly, to boot.

"This," said Francesca, "is Prince SavvY of Smug.
He's addicted to FASHION; he thinks it's a drug!
He's swisher than SWANK and he's slicker than *sleek*!
His clothes are so modern, they come from next week!"

"For real," said the prince, through the veil of his wig.
"This outfit comes straight from the future, you dig?
In my kingdom, they call me 'the Captain of Snazz'!
And I listen to *only* the hippest of jazz!"

To prove it, the prince did a bit of a scat.
He went, "Skoo-bibbly-doo!" then he tipped up his hat.

"Oooooh!" said the revelers, clearly impressed.
"He's so fresh!" they exclaimed.
"Just look how he's dressed!"
"We WANT it!" they cried. "We'll WEAR it!" they brayed.
(These sorts of people were easily swayed.)

"Fresh?!" asked Prince Hep, for he wasn't convinced.
"No offense, but that outfit? It's ... s*tinky*." He winced.

"Wait," said *Miss Ruby*. "I've heard of this, yes.
It's a little bit ... *pungent*, but nevertheless

it's making a statement. It's **BOLD**—it's risqué!
A revolution in FASHION, I might even say.

"Though *some* might not wear it, I certainly would.
It's 'organic fashion' and I think it's quite good.
And *since* I'm the Spiffian maven of style,
you must do as I say," she said, with a smile.

She turned from Prince Hep and, facing the crowd,
she spread her arms **wide** and shouted aloud:
"Listen to me, my *delectable* friends!
Prince Savvy of Smug is a setter of trends!

"His apparel, I realize, is rather surreal,
but it does have an odd sort of modern appeal.
So hear this, my followers: Starting today,
we shall dress in the very same, sumptuous way!

"We shall give this advancement in FASHION a shot.
We shall dress up in leaves! In fungus and rot!
Our pants shall be **mossy**, with festering threads!
We shall have only *foul-smelling* fruit on our heads!"

"Wait—just a moment," said Prince Savvy of Smug.

(From the tip of his nose, he peeled off a slug.)
"It seems all you want is my clothing!" he cried.
"But what about *me*, the person inside?"

Sadly, this comment was largely ignored.
The guests who were watching appeared to be bored.
The whole of the crowd, this exalted elite,
they stood there and sheepishly shuffled their feet.

It was Ruby, at last, who had something to say.
"We LOVE it," she said, in a flattering way.
"Don't you see? It's a dashing, delicious new fad.
It might be the best one that we've ever had!
No matter the co$t, whatever it's worth,
we'll follow this trend to the ends of the earth!"

"I see," said Prince SAVVY. "If that's all you want,
some crazy new FASHION to flog and to flaunt,
if you only want clothes for your fashion boutiques,
then fine! You can take what I'm wearing—
IT REEKS!"

He slipped off his leaves, and the peat of his pants.
He stripped off the fungus, the branches, the plants.

He whipped off his wig, and the fruit off his head.
"There! It's all yours. You can have it," he said.

The Spiffians gaped. They giggled, as well.
For the prince had no clothes. He was au naturel. ♥
He wore only ♥nderpants, printed with hearts. ♥ ♥
(They covered up only his naughtiest parts.) ♥ ♥ ♥

"How uncouth!" cried the crowd.
"How vulgar! How rude!
Look at him there! Why, he's practically nude!"
It was not only that. There was also this fact:
"Prince SAVVY of Smug"—it was only an act.

It was PUGGLY, of course, dressed up in disguise,
which I'm sure isn't really a massive surprise.
He had mimicked the SHAMAN,
and the way that he spoke.
The only thing missing was the pipe and the smoke.

"Let's leave them," said Fran to her Spudlian friend,
"to the 'fruits' of their latest, lamentable trend.
Tell my father," she said, "wherever he is,
I'm through with this Spiffian kingdom of his.

I've decided, in fact, this kingdom's a dud.
I'm through with the SPIFFS. I'm moving to SPUD!"

So turning her back, with no more to say,
she took Puggly's arm and

she   *led*

him   away.

Together they left, by the palace's door,
in **pajamas** and ♥ndies ... and nothing else more.

CHAPTER 10
over-Chewed Gum

HEN Francesca arrived

at the palace of Spud, with its one
lonely turret and meadows of mud,
she could tell that the kingdom was shabby, at best,
but at least no one cared about how she was dressed.

To Frannie's surprise, PUGGLY told her to wait
when the twosome arrived at the palace's gate.
"Here we are," he said meekly. "Can I give you a tour?
I could show you the **mud** that we keep on the
moor."

Frannie declined, with a shake of her head,
"Could I maybe see something less . . . muddy, instead?
Maybe your books? Do you keep them up there?"

                                            air.
                                    in the
                            rose
                    that
                turret
She referred to the

"Books?" Puggly mumbled. "They're not up there, no."
As he spoke, his voice was halting and low.
"They're in . . . Library Hall, which is way at the back.
We have tons of them there. In stack after stack."

As Puggly was speaking, he seemed oddly resigned.
He appeared to be nervous, uncertain of mind.

"You okay?" Frannie asked. "You seem overly coy.
It's your home. You ought to be jumping for joy."
Then it dawned on Francesca, the problem at hand.
"Oh, I get it!" she nodded. "Yeah, I understand.

"It's clear to me now—as clear as a bell!

I'd be hesitant, too. I'd be worried as well.
I'd be blushing, embarrassed, my confidence gone,
if all that I had were my ♥nderpants on."

Puggly looked down at what little he wore.
Then, though he hadn't been blushing before,
from the waist of his undies to the top of his head,
every inch of his skin turned amazingly red.

Puggly said, "No! It's not that at all,
but I'm not sure we'll get to see Library Hall.
See, I gave up my crown at the party tonight.
My people might find that a bit ... impolite.

"They might be quite angry, at least a bit miffed.
I guess you could say I've created a rift.
And so ... " he went on, his voice papery thin,
"THERE'S KIND OF A CHANCE THEY WON'T LET US IN."

The moment he said this,
there came a great **CLANK!**
From over the moat, from the opposite bank,
the drawbridge was lowered, coming down with a thud,
as the gates opened up to the palace of **SPUD**.

A crowd had assembled on the palace's lawn,
every Spudlian face looking dour, withdrawn,
and some of them bitter, indignant, *severe*.
"It's him!" someone snorted. "Prince Poopy is here."

The Spuds were irate. They had every right.
After all, they had heard what had happened that night.
The driver had told them. He said, "*Puggly resigned!*
The Prince of the **SPUDS** has left us behind!"

What made it worse, made it hurt all the more,
was the very same thing had happened before.
It was just like King Walter,
when he gave them the s*lip*,
to go run a salon in the **Kingdom of HIP**.

So the news about Puggly had caused quite a stir!
Just imagine how deeply upset they all were.

As Puggly and Frannie crossed over the moat,
the prince was quite nervous, a **lump** in his throat.
The farther he walked, the more **lumpy** it got.
It felt like his tonsils were tied in a knot.
Halfway across, he was taken aback.

For guess who was there, at the front of the pack?
It was someone quite old (but known to be wise),
despite having clouds in the both of her eyes.

That's right: his great-granny. But instead of relieved,
the wrinkly old woman looked rather aggrieved.

"**PUGG-LY!**" she hollered.
"I am **FLIPPING MY LID!**
Is it true what they're saying?! Is it true what you did?"
She pointed at Puggly with the end of her cane.
"Start talking, my boy! You had better explain!"

"Uh, I . . ." Puggly spluttered, but stopped out of shame.
The end of his sentence? Well, it just never came.

       steps, the **SHAMAN** was perched.
   the
  on
Up
"Where were you, **P-MAN?**
We searched and we searched!
And then we find out that you're callin' it quits.

No way, little prince! **Man**, that's just the pits!
Some people might even think it was *rude*.
Cuz we love ya, **P-MAN**! Don't *abdicate*, dude."

Puggly faltered again, as he tried to convey
exactly what happened, in a meaningful way.
But the sound he produced was more like a wheeze,
like the SQUEAK of a mouse—with a mouthful of
CHEESE.

As such, it was good he'd brought Frannie along.
"Wait!" She stepped forward.
"You've got Puggly all wrong!
I know that I've known him for only a day,
but he's such a nice guy! So all I can say,
is maybe you're angry, which is perfectly fine,
but you ought to be mad at that *kingdom* of mine.
And not merely the SPIFFS, but all of the rest.
They were *all* making fun of how Puggly was dressed."

As she said this, the crowd appeared to be quelled.
Their sense of resentment was slowly dispelled.
Their bodies relaxed. Their teeth came unclenched.
The thirst of their tempers was quietly quenched.

What once had been anger had started to melt.
After all, every **SPUD** knew just how it felt
to be slandered, insulted, or simply ignored,
to be told that their clothing was always deplored.

It all made the prince feel a little less bleak,
and so, once again, he was able to speak.
"I'm sorry," he murmured. "It was never my plan
to upset anybody, when all this began."

He tried to explain. He quickly described
how the guests at the party had jabbered and jibed.
How *Miss Ruby* herself had insulted his wig,
and told him his crown "wasn't fit for a pig."

How it made him feel worthless, like over-chewed gum,
like a big, **bursting** boil on an elephant's bum.
That's how he felt: unwanted, naïve.
After hearing it all, he just wanted to leave.

So of course he ran off. What else could he do?
Wouldn't anyone else have *run* away too?

"But I'm sorry," he said, "if I let you all down.

I should never have *ever* relinquished my crown.
It's a sensitive issue," Prince Puggly confessed,
"and I quite understand if you're not too impressed.

"It *might've* been better to hurry back here.
It's here, among **SPUDS**, where I've nothing to FEAR.
But had I returned, you shouldn't forget,
Francesca and I would never have met."

He smiled at the *princess*, who stood by his side.
Her smile, in return, was equally **wide**.

"It's true," Frannie added. "Prince Puggly is right.
If we hadn't run into each other tonight,
it would have been awful. We would never have got
the chance to devise such a masterful plot!"

She explained what they did, their ridiculous feat:
How they'd sewn a disguise out of fungus and peat,
out of TWIGS, out of **moss**, out of mushrooms and MOLD,
and soon, the whole laughable story was told.

And oh, what a story! So silly! So daft!
(The Spudlians loved it. They laughed and they
laughed!)

Even Puggly's great-granny was bursting with mirth.
She giggled and jiggled her elderly girth.
She was laughing so hard it looked like a dance.
In fact, she was this close to wetting her pants.

(But she didn't.)

Instead, she dabbed at her eyes.
"It's disgusting," she chuckled, "but *what* a disguise!"

"**Right on**," said the Shaman.
                          "What you pulled was cool.
You made that *La Rue* lady look like a fool!
So, **P-MAN**, I think we forgive you," he said.
"And there's something that's missing on top of your
head!"

                          great height,
                    turret's
                to the
            up
The **SHAMAN** looked
where the driver who drove to the party that night
was hanging the crown by the crook of his thumbs.
"You ready?" he cried. "Okay! Here it comes!"

Then, as before, with a pulley and crank,
the crown floated down, with a cl*ink* and a cl*ank*.
As if on a fishing rod (with the strangest of bait),

the crown landed softly on Prince Puggly's pate.

"WHOOPEE!" cried the SPUDS.
"Hurrah and hooray!
Our prince has returned—after going a s t r a y !"

Francesca, however, wasn't quite so enthused.
"Hmm . . ." she said slowly, a little bemused.

She cocked her head sideways. She squinted her eyes.
"Are you sure," she inquired, "that crown is your size?
It might be just me, or perhaps it's your wig,
but from here, it looks like your crown is . . . *too big*."

Puggly's great-granny replied with a smile.
"It's fine," she responded. "That's just our style.
We happen to like our crowns big, I suppose.
Anyway, he'll look better . . . once he puts on some
clothes."

Again, Puggly's skin turned the rosiest pink.
He wished he could hide; he wished he could shrink.
He nervously giggled and started to sweat.
"Oh, yeah," he burst out. "How could I forget?"

Francesca said, "*Ugh*! Puggly, c'mon.
Let's go inside. You can put something on.
Also, I can *finally* get to explore
that Library Hall you mentioned before."

They drew *up the drawbridge* and all went inside:
a wrinkly old granny, with a lim*p* in her stride;
a **BELL-BOTTOMED** guru, with a turban on top;
a **pajama**-clad *princess*, with hair like a mop.

The servants, as well, and all of the crowd,
they parted, they stood, they quietly bowed.
Then into the palace they began to proceed
with a newly crowned, half-naked prince in the lead . . .

CHAPTER 11
the Strangest, Most Curious Coat

After
bathing and dressing,
when Puggly was done,
his clothing was perfect. He was
second-to-none!
("Perfect," of course, in a Spudlian mode:

like a b**o**m**b** full of color had come to explode.)

"C'mon, Frannie," he said, "let me show you the Hall,
the shelves and the books—I'll show you them all!"

The princess, at first, was rather beguiled.
She wandered the stacks. She chuckled and smiled.
"Amazing!" she said, reading spine after spine.
"Your collection is nearly as mammoth as mine!"

Nearly, however, was the pivotal word.
As she said it, something surprising occurred.
She suddenly frowned. "This is awful," she said.
"Every book you've got here, I've already read!"

She began to feel dizzy. She started to sway. It felt like her insides were floating away. The room started spinning. It shimmered and swirled. "Have I read," she cried out, "EVERY WORD IN THE WORLD?!"

(No. She had not.)

There were *plenty* more left.
There was no need to act so absurdly bereft.

"Excuse me," said someone, just off to the rear.
The voice was so soft it was tricky to hear.
"You need something to read? Did I hear you right?
I think there's a chance I can help with your plight."

"Who said that?" asked Frannie, for she was surprised.
In the corner, she saw that the shadows disguised
a very small room, like a closet or booth.
(It was more like a *crypt*, to tell you the truth.)

"It's my granny," said Puggly. "You met her before.
To be honest, she's not really part of the tour.
She says that she's writing her memoirs back there.
If she's telling the truth, it's a lengthy affair!

"For *years*, she's been scribbling, like she'll never be done,
on so many notebooks, they must weigh a ton!
Though I can't say what's in them, I have to confess.
The ravings of a lonely old woman, I guess."

"**BALDERDASH**, boy!" was his granny's reply.
"*Lonely old ravings?!* Why, that is a lie!
It's not merely scribbling! It's not '*blah-blah-blah* . . . '
It's the whole of my life! It's the legend of *moi*!"

She peeked out at Frannie and beckoned her close.
"Come here," she summoned. "I'll give you a dose.
I've got it all here, every salient breath,

every tri^{u}m^{ph} and f$_{a_{i_{l_{u_{r_e}}}}}$ from birth until death!"

Francesca stepped forward, peering into the gloom.
What she saw was a desk in a **SHADOWY ROOM**.
"Those scrolls," she said sadly. "There's only a few.
I could read that whole stack in a minute or two."

Puggly's granny said, "*These?* I wrote them just now.
This is all of the paper my space would allow.
But a *great* many more can be easily found,
in my Biography Vault, under the ground."

"Wait," Puggly sputtered. "Is there something I missed?
"*A Biography Vault?* Does that really exist?"

His granny retorted, "Of course it does, boy!
I love it down there. It's my ultimate joy.
Didn't you know?" she asked, with a smirk.
"There're tombs down below,
where
     I've
        hidden
           my work!"

With that, his great-granny leaned back on her seat.
With the help of her cane, she rose to her feet.
From a drawer, she retrieved a jangle of keys.
"This way," she said, with a cough and a *wheeze*.

She tottered unsteadily over the floor,
to the rear of the room, to a **SHADOWY DOOR**.
She opened it up. It led to a ledge.
Slowly, the woman limped out to the edge.

She paused, then she flipped on a switch to ignite:
Torches! They kindled with flickering light.

Below them spread out a most marvelous space,
with shelves running madly all over the place!

Like a miniature city, a miraculous sprawl,
it was *ten times* the size of Library Hall!

Puggly was shocked, from his eyebrows on down.
(They shot ^{up} so high, they were crowding his crown!)
"All this? By yourself?!" Prince Puggly began.
"But when? It seems so impossible, Gran!

"You had to have started this *ages* ago.
But where did you HIDE IT, is what I'd like to know!
How is it possible? How could I miss
my very own gran, writing something like this?!"

The old woman smiled. "It's not really so hard.
It's easy, in fact, in a certain regard.
All it takes is hard work, by night and by day,
in a quiet, collected and diligent way."

Yet still, poor old Puggly was taken aback.
"Now, wait," he insisted. "We lived in a *shack*!
Were you writing this then, when we lived on the moors?
How is it possible all of it's yours?!"

"It is," shrugged his gran, in a casual way.

She seemed unconcerned, and even blasé.
"*Of course* it's all mine. What's the matter with you?
That shack had a cellar . . . I thought that you knew.

"If not, I suppose it might strike you as weird,
but that shack was far bigger than at first it appeared.
The basement was **MASSIVE**,
you can take it from me.
It was fairly impressive, architecturally.

"My memoir's been there since before you were born.
That's why the pages are tattered and worn.
When we moved to the palace, I wanted them near,
so I sent every carriage, to bring it all here.

"So that's how it happened," the woman professed.
"I wrote everything down! I'm a little obsessed.
I might even be crackers," she said, with a wink.
"I'm an '*autobiographicaholic*,' I think."

"That's for sure," Frannie said. She completely concurred.
"But what you just said? I don't think that's a word."

The old woman nodded. "That proves it! *Oh, yes!*

I could tell you were bookish, I have to confess.
And as you can see, I've got just what you need.
From now on, my girl, you'll have *plenty* to read ..."

For days, Frannie lived in a book-lover's dream:
Words—in a seemingly infinite stream!
What Puggly's great-granny had told her was true.
She had m$o^{u^{n^{t^{a^i}}}}$ns to read, and all of it new!

The woman had lived an incredible life.
There were soarings of joy! There were crashes of strife!
There was lyrical poetry! Tales within tales!
Mystery? Humor? It had them in bales!

Frannie had never had so much to read.
(The hoary old crone was *prolific*, indeed.)
Yet something was missing. She wasn't sure what,
but Frannie could feel it,

                        deep

                            down

                                in her gut.

It wasn't the book that was making her blue.
It wasn't a *what*. It, in fact, was a *who*.
The person who tugged at the back of her mind
was *her father*, of course! She had left him
behind.

Although she was happy to settle in SPUD,
a strong sense of longing was haunting her blood.
My father, she thought, I hope he's all right.
Perhaps I should visit him later tonight . . .

Ironically, as she was having this thought,
Puggly came running, looking rather distraught.
"Francesca," he said, "there's a man at the moat!
He's dressed in the *strangest*, most curious coat!

"Yet the outfit is somewhat familiar to me.
I wore one myself, to a certain degree.
It's a coat made of leaves, but it's crawling with bugs!
And his pants!
They're all mossy and SLIMY with slugs!
He has the things crawling all over the place.
In fact, there's so many, you can't
see his face!"

"**Slugs?**" asked Francesca. "And **SLIMY**, as well?
Disgusting! I can only imagine the smell!"

"True," Puggly said, "but there's also the *sound*.
He's ranting and raving and stomping the ground.
His behavior, quite frankly, has left me perplexed,
and whoever he is, he is *terribly vexed*."

"Okay," said Francesca, "this might sound naïve,
but, Puggly . . . why don't you ask him to leave?"

"*Because*," Puggly answered, "what else could I do?
This stranger? He says he's related to you!
When he said that, I assumed he was mad.
But you know what he told me?
He said he's your dad!"

Yes, it would seem that King Dandy was there.
He still remained wigless, without any hair,
but his clothes were exactly as Puggly explained:
They were sloppy and **SLIMY** and stinky and stained.

above.

ramparts

the

to

"My daughter!" he called
"Are you there? I've been such a dullard, my LOVE!
I may have been 'king,' I might have been 'chief,'
but for ages I've given you nothing but grief!

"But once you were gone, I knew it was true:
What matters the most—oh, Frannie, it's you!
So I might've been slow, but now I can see:
Pajamas with boats? They're okay by me."

In the Spudlian turret, Francesca was there.
She smiled from its balcony, up in the air.
She was happy to hear what her father had said
(she just hoped he hadn't gone soft in the head).

"Daddy!" she called to him, down

by

the

moat.

She suddenly had a great lump in her throat.

From out of one eye came the drip of a tear.
"I *missed* you!" she sobbed. "I'm so glad that you're here!"

Then turning to Puggly and beaming a grin,
she said, "It's my father! You *must* let him in!"
"I *would*," Puggly answered, with a bit of a scowl.
"But his clothes! Let's face it, Francesca, *they're foul*!"

When Frannie heard this, she was rather dismayed.
"Puggly," she said. "You're wrong, I'm afraid.
We *must* let him in. I mean, isn't it clear?
Have you really not spotted the irony here?
Are you truly prepared to deny his request,
for no better reason than ... *how he is dressed*?!"

Puggly thought about this. He could see she was right.
He felt a bit guilty, and even contrite.
He yelled to his guards, "His Kingship awaits!
Lower the *drawbridge* and open the gates!"

They heaved at the lever and, turning the crank,
the drawbridge was cast to the opposite bank.

The king crossed the moat at a lumbering trot,
dripping with mushrooms and fungus and rot.

Delighted, Francesca felt almost sublime.
She leapt down the steps, going two at a time.
She welcomed the king with a cozy embrace,
but ended the hug with a **slug** on her face.

"This is unpleasant," she said, with a sigh,
when she noticed the creature, just under her eye.
It clung to her cheek like a **SILVERY** drip.
It crawled down her nose to the top of her lip.

She put up her hand, with no lack of aplomb,
and peeled it away, with a finger and thumb.
Without even an *"EEW!"* or an *"ICK!"* or a *"BLEK!"*
she returned it to the king, on the side of his neck.

"You realize," she said, "you are covered in **dirt**.
There're more bugs on your back than actual shirt.
And I nearly just suffered a slug up my nose.
So tell us: WHY ARE YOU
WEARING THOSE
CLOTHES?!"

Chapter 12
spreadin' the Love

"**Well,**" said King Dandy, "what else could I do? It's because of that harpy, Miss Ruby LaRue.

She considers this 'hip,'" he said, with a hiss. "Every SPIFF in the kingdom wears something like this!"

Prince Puggly had joined them. He was listening, too.
"You wear it?" he asked. "Is that really true?"

"It's true!" cried the king. "Believe it or not,
they made *everyone* dress in that fungus and rot!
They said, 'Oh, it's so snazzy! Oh, it's so cool!'
Well, it wasn't! I tell you, that clothing was cruel!

"But if *Miss Ruby* likes it, they think it's all chic!
Only none of it lasts for more than a week.
Our clothing is rotting right off of our backs,
and I think I have *worms* living under my slacks!"

Fran looked at Puggly, and he looked at her.
It was clear to them both, they each could infer:
This ridiculous trend was because of their prank.
Every SPIFF in that kingdom had Puggly to thank.

"Wait," said Francesca. "I don't understand.
Why is this clothing in sudden demand?
'Prince SAVVY of Smug' was meant as a laugh,
a joke we came up with on Puggly's behalf.

"That's why he dressed in so awful a style.
We made sure it was something especially vile.
But how can a passion for fashion persist
when the person who started it doesn't exist?"

"*Because,*" said the King, with a look of malaise.
"To *Miss Ruby,* it's not just a fad or a phase.
This 'organic' nonsense? She wants it to stay.
What she wants is a trend that won't go away.

"For it's not about FASHION *at all* anymore!
It's all about how much will sell in a store.
And when clothes made of fungus are all that you've got,
then one day you're dressed, the next one you're not.

"Your clothes rot away 'til you're utterly bare.
You look down for your breeches,
but they simply aren't there!
You're completely unveiled! Without even a stitch!
It's no wonder it's making *Miss Ruby* so rich.

"Because suddenly, there you are, walking about,
with only one sleeve and your bum hanging out!

So of course you run back to *Miss Ruby*, and then:
You buy the same outfit all over again!

"This 'FASHION' caught on like an awful disease,
like a virulent flu—from one massive sneeze!
Every kingdom but this one is caught in its grip,
from the **Kingdom of SPIFF** to the **Kingdom of HIP**!

"So that's why I came. I decided to quit.
I told them, I'm finished! I'm leaving! That's it!
Clothes such as these I could *never* endorse.
Abdication, therefore, was my only recourse."

"You quit?" asked Francesca. "You're no longer king?
You're tossing your hat—I mean, *crown*—in the ring?"

"Indeed," said the hitherto king of the SPIFFS.
"I'll never return to those miserable cliffs!
And you know?" he continued. "I think I should add:
This **kingdom of SPUD**? It's not really so bad . . ."

"But wait!" said the king, "there's one other thing."
He opened his satchel, untying the string.
"I imagine it's something you probably missed.

It's yours, after all. It's called *Oliver Twist.*"

The moment she saw it, Francesca said, "*Wow!*
Oh, Dad, you're amazing! I can finish it now!"
She accepted the book, held it close to her chest.
"Thank you!" she gushed. "You're the absolute best!"

Her father smiled meekly. "I'm sorry," he said.
He absently fondled the bald of his head.
"It's not just the book. It's not just the clothes.
The reason I came . . . it's neither of those.

"Not books and not FASHION. That's not why I'm here.
I came here *for you.* My daughter. My dear.
I no longer care about little chapeaus.
If we can't be together, *who cares* about clothes?!"

The princess felt happiness t^{i}ck$_l$e her he♥rt.
"We'll live here," she exclaimed, "so we won't be
apart!"

Then, like her father before her, she paused.
"I'm sorry," she added, "for the trouble I caused.
I might be a little too stubborn, too stiff.

Or maybe that's just part of being a SPIFF."

She regarded her father with a curious smile.
"I was thinking," she said. "Perhaps for a while,
maybe, just once, I could test it, you know?
I could dress up—*just once*—in a dress with a bow."

At this, the king laughed. "Don't be silly, my dear.
Dresses?" he whispered. "So *very* last year."
                    up his daughter and gave her a hug.
Then he picked
It was joyous, euphoric—and LOVINGLY snug!

"Oh, boy!" Puggly sniffled. "A reunion! Right here!
I'm a bit overwhelmed, and I'm being sincere!"

(He was.)

The proof was right there on his cheeks:
Tears of joy, dri_pping down in two blu_bbery streaks.

He couldn't just stand there. What else could he do?
That hug was so lovely, he wanted one, too.
So he slipped in between with relative ease,

for a cozy (but clumsy) triangular **SQUEEZE.**

"**Groovy!** Right on!" said a voice from above.
"Nothin' beats huggin' when you're spreadin' the love."

Puggly looked up from his three-sided hug.
There was the **SHAMAN**'s magnanimous mug.
In a window above them, the man could be seen
peering down from the turret, looking calm and serene.

He appeared to be holding a watering can.
"Don't mind me," said the Shaman.
"You keep huggin', my man."
Reaching over his turban, all fluffy and red,
he watered the daisy that grew on his head.

"So much **looove**," he went on.
"You're blowin' my mind!
That hug is the ultimate! It's one of a kind!
This calls for a banquet! We'll celebrate, since
it's a *double reunion*, for a king and a prince.

And you know what that means? It's as good as it gets!
It means DOUBLE THE PARTY, for us dudes
and dudettes!"

Puggly gazed upward, so beaming with hope,
so full of excitement, he hardly could cope.
In his mind he could see it: a gala affair!
This time would be different.
All his friends would be there!

"A PARTY?!" he wondered.
"With streamers galore?
With kazoos and confetti? With all that and more!
With tinsel and music and ... even BALLOONS!?!
And dancing! To the latest, most popular tunes!"

"You got it, P-MAN," was the Shaman's reply.
"Balloons and confetti in DOUBLE SUPPLY!
Don't worry, P-Man, we'll do it up right.
And here's something else. That PARTY's ...

TONIGHT!"

For Puggly, of course, this was mind-blowing news.
That's exactly what happened: His brain blew a fuse.
His eyes started reeling and casting about.
His mouth opened up, but only drool drib_bled out.

Then he fainted, out cold, his world turning black.
He went limp as a noodle and **fell flat on his back** . . .

CHAPTER 13
our Man of the Mud

When

Puggly awoke, he saw flashes of light.
They jabbed at his eyelids, painfully bright . . .

He heard music, as well: the lilting of lutes;
the grumble of tubas; the whistle of flutes;
and perhaps—just perhaps—the bray of bassoons.
Then he opened his eyes to see only . . . **BALLOONS!**

"I think this is it," he whispered, and then
he came *verrry* close to fainting again.

(But he didn't.)

Although he was right on the verge,
he bravely was able to fight off the urge.
He shook off his stupor. He was no longer dazed.
He instead was astounded. The prince was *amazed*!

He was slum_{ped} on his throne like a half-empty sack,
an uncomfortable slouch in the curve of his back.
Every **SPUD** in the kingdom was with him, as well.
As he **STRAIGHTENED** himself, Prince Puggly could tell:

He was smack in the midst of a special event.
There was singing—and *dancing*! He knew what that
meant.

A *PARTY!* he thought. Amazing! At last!
By the look of things, everyone's having a blast!
There he was, in the midst of a Spudlian ball.
For a moment, he sat there, just watching it all.

There was Francesca. She danced with her dad.
His outfit had changed, and now he was clad
in **SPUDLIAN** clothes, in trousers that drooped
(as if, in the back, he had recently pooped).

Meanwhile, the **SHAMAN** was also on hand.
He was up on the stage, with the Spudlian band.
He wore big platform heels and a flowery suit,
and was **rockin'** it out, on electrical lute!

                affixed to a wall.
         a banner,
      was
   above
Up
It said, in huge letters, stupendously tall:

WELCOME BACK, PUGGLY!
OUR MAN OF THE MUD!
(AND TO FRANNIE'S POP, TOO:
HEY, WELCOME TO SPUD.)
NOW, GET UP AND DANCE! IT'S A PARTY, YOU BET!
IT'S A DOUBLE REUNION! A FEAST AND A FÊTE!

Prince Puggly was pleased! He admired the crowd.
He gazed at their outfits. So garish! So loud!
He beamed as they danced in their fanciest shoes.
A few of them even were B L O W I N G k a z o o s !

To top it all off, a **BALLOON** had come loose,
   floating
                  down
         like a
                  feather
         plucked
                  out of a goose.
It tumbled.
         It wafted.
                  It finally d
                                 r
                                   o
                                     p
                                       p
                                         e
                                           d,
down on the crest of his crown . . . where it popped.

"He's awake!" someone shouted.

"It's true!" someone said.
"He's coming around!"
"He's back from the dead!"

Then nobody spoke. Instead, THEY ALL FROZE.
The people stopped dancing and tapping their toes.
The Shaman stopped strumming, in the midst of a riff.
There was no sound at all.

Not a cough.

Not a sniff.

Faced with this silence, as still as a grave,
Prince Puggly stood up. He gave them a wave.

"HOORAY!" cried the Spuds.
They shouted. They roared.
They showed off how deeply their prince was adored.

At last, when the cheers were beginning to wane,
the **SHAMAN** stepped up,
with a glass of champagne.
"Hey, P-MAN," he said. "If you're in the mood,

would'ja give us a speech? Like, say somethin',
dude!"

A speech? Puggly thought. I'll give it a try
(in spite of his throat going horribly dry).

"We **SPUDS**," he began, "we're not really revered.
Other kingdoms around think we're all a bit weird.
To them, it would seem, we're not '*stylish*' enough.
They want us to dress up in trendier stuff.
Well, to me, you look great! There's nothing amiss.
I'm proud to be prince of a kingdom like this!

"A kingdom where each of us looks like a kook!
Where our socks and our shoes are the color of puke!
Where our riffles and ruffles are lacking finesse!
Where our powdery wigs are a wonderful mess!
Where the backs of our breeches sag down in the butt!
And if they don't like it, then we say:
SO WHAT?!!"

Prince Puggly was ready to say something more,
when a stranger appeared, to darken the door.
(And when I said, "stranger," as I did so, just then,
I meant it. That was no slip of my pen.)

This stranger got right to the root of the word.
He looked very strange. He looked rather absurd.
For all he was wearing, like Puggly before,
were Y-fronted underpants . . . and nothing else more.

Unlike Puggly, however, these undies were tight.
They didn't have he♥rts; they were brilliantly white.

In the silence that followed, it was Frannie who spoke.
She said to the stranger, "Are you stealing our joke?
The whole 'undie' thing? I think that you'll find
we tried that already. You're a little behind."

"*No!*" cried the stranger. He was standing his ground.
"I'm serious, here! I'm not joking around!
In the place where I'm from, the only clothing they sell
is rotten and soggy—and infested, as well!

"You can take it from me, it's appalling to wear!
There were *beetles*," he said. "*Nearly ruined my hair!*"

His hair. Why, of course! That was the clue!
It was then, all at once, every **SPUDLIAN** knew
who was standing before them at the palace's door.

(How was it, they wondered, they hadn't noticed before?)

"KING WALTER?!"
they cried.

"Can it actually be?!"

(It could.)

But he'd changed, to a certain degree.
How had he changed? It was slight, I suppose,
but I think it had something to do with his nose . . .

In any case, yes, the **SPUDS** had it right,
but their previous king was a *sorrowful* sight.
He was haggard and haunted, a little too THIN,
and some sort of rash was afflicting his skin.

From his undies on up, he was blotchy and red.
"I'm *allergic* to 'organic fashion,'" he said.
Yet his hair was untouched. Why, it looked rather nice.
A big, blond bouffant! It was plump and precise.

As the Spudlians gazed at that champion coif,
they remembered *the reason* their king had r u n off.

"Wait a second!" they shouted. "Perhaps you recall,
not long ago, you *abandoned* us all!
We woke up one morning and—POOF!—you were gone.
You left us, remember? To run a salon!"

"It's true," Walter nodded. "I had to, you see?
Being 'King of the **SPUDS**?' That wasn't for me.

I'm *quite* good with scissors, as I'm sure you can tell.
So that had a certain advantage, as well.
But look what their clothing has done to my skin!
Please! C'mon guys, could you let me back in?"

In response, the whole crowd had one thing to say:
"We no longer need 'kings.' So please: GO AWAY!"

"Wait!" Walter cried. "I don't wanna be king!
I told you already, that isn't my thing.
Just lend me some ointment and vitamin pills.
I'll open a barbershop, up in the hills."

"**No way,**" said the Spuds.
"You are not what we like.
You and your hairdo can go take a hike.
That's right, you heard us. Now, leave us alone.
Besides . . . we've got someone new on the throne."

stood up, as if rising on cue.
Prince Puggly
As he did, the whole crowd separated in two.
The prince began looking down the length of the aisle.
When his eyes met Francesca's, he gave her a smile.

Then he said to his people: "Is that really fair?
Do we really choose kings on account of their hair?
It just isn't right. After all, if we do,
then we're all just as bad as *Miss Ruby LaRue*."

"Besides," he went on, "the guy's covered in hives.
So everyone—STOP! For once in our lives,
we're dropping the focus on collars and sleeves,
on fabrics and patterns and stitches and weaves!

"Every kingdom's gone mad! In even our own,
our fixation on fashion is overly blown.
When it comes to our clothes, we ought to be free,
and wear what we want, unconditionally.

"Whether wild or refined, whether subtle or brash,
you can wear it—as long as you don't get a rash.
What's really so wrong with SPIFFIAN style?
Perhaps we could try it, just once in a while.

"And they could try ours! Is that really so strange?
I'm sure we have fashion advice to exchange.
It ought to be *fun*. It's what FASHION is for!
But that's *all* it is. Just fun. Nothing more.

"It shouldn't—*it mustn't*—cause anyone strife.
C'mon, guys, let's face it. There's a lot more to life."

These words from the throne had dramatic effect.
The **SPUDS** could all see that their prince was correct.
They said sorry to Walter; the man was consoled,
as they welcomed him back to the Spudlian fold.

To Puggly, the **SHAMAN** said,
"**Dude!** Wicked speech.
Congrats, little **P-MAN**, on healin' the breech."
He reached up for the banner hanging over his head.
Crossing out the word "DOUBLE," he wrote "TRIPLE"
instead . . .

"Oh, thank you!" said Walter, the hitherto king.
"This rash I've contracted? It really does sting."
So the Spuds gathered round him, with cottony swabs,
and smeared him in ointment, in generous globs.

"Feels great!" Walter cooed. "Lemme tell you, it's bliss!
I just hope you've got a whole barrel of this.
You see," he went on, beginning to swoon,
"I think you might need a lot more of it soon . . . "

It was Frannie who first understood what he meant.
"Outside!" she told Puggly—and to the windows they went.

In an instant, they saw that the princess was right.
There were all sorts of people,

coming out of the night.

They *staggered* like zombies,

stumbling over the ground,

people from every last kingdom around.

From the **Kingdom of** SPIFF, the **Kingdom of** sleek;
from the **Kingdom of** HIP and the **Kingdom of** chic;
from the **Kingdom of** *Swish*, of **Mod** and of FAD!
As Walter predicted, they all looked pretty bad.

Their skin was all red and their clothes were all gone.
Every one of them only had underwear on!

"We're sorry," they called, "we made fun of you guys!
We can sort of see now, that wasn't so wise.
We know we all acted like a whole bunch of *schmoes*,
but please: COULD WE MAYBE JUST
BORROW SOME CLOTHES?!"

"**Groovy**," said the **SHAMAN**.
"Bring 'em in! Bring 'em all!
"Let 'em in and let's **PARTY**! We'll all have a ball!
Cuz no matter what happens, I know this much is true:
We're gonna party, right now, like it's 1602!"

Meanwhile, in an alcove, at the back of the room,
hidden from sight in the **SHADOWS** and **GLOOM**,
one foggy old person had witnessed it all:
the jumble and joy of a Spudlian Ball!

This person just smiled. She nodded, and then:
For the very last time, she picked up her pen . . .

So they all lived in **SPUD**, and there they remain,
where Puggly the prince still continues to reign,
where he usually dresses a bit like a nut,
in polka-dot breeches that sag in the butt.
Where a *princess* in PJs is free to proceed
to follow her dreams—to read and to read.
Where the princess's dad became less of a prig,
and (briefly) considered a **SPUDLIAN** wig.

Where close to the palace, way up in the hills,
a barber, renowned for his scissoring skills,
can offer you any old style you could want
(but his favorite, of course, is a massive bouffant).

And where, if you visit, it often is said,
there's a man with a daisy on top of his head.
He wears **BELL-BOTTOMED** breeches,
a flowery suit,
and he'll teach you some chords on electrical lute . . .

And so, my good reader, believe it or not,
we have just about come to the end of the plot.
All that remains is the usual stuff:
the pithy conclusion, the summary fluff.

But as for a moral, what can I say?
Some tired old chestnut? Some common cliché?
No, I don't think so. Those lessons and rules,
in my humble opinion, are only for fools.
Yet I realize it's something some readers may miss.
And so, here we go. The moral is this:

If you happen to follow some popular trend,
be careful. It leads to an unhappy end.
You may be accepted, you may knock 'em dead,
but you'll also have festering fruit on your head.

But wait! you insist. There's still something more.
There's a pertinent matter you shouldn't ignore!

Ah, yes, my good reader, I see what you mean.
Your skills of perception are certainly keen.

You're correct. There is something I've so far concealed.
There's one bit remaining I haven't revealed.
It's about Puggly's invite that came in the mail,
near the start of this rather meandering tale.

The question itself is a question of who.
Who sent it? you wonder. I'll give you a clue:
It was someone quite old, but known to be wise,
someone with clouds in the both of her eyes.

Those eyes are right here. They're inside of my head,
and the last of my memoir is what you just read.
So, with a wink from this foggy old eye,
I bid you farewell, and I bid you . . .

goodbye.

ACKNOWLEDGMENTS

This book would not have been possible without the efforts of many incredible people. My sincere thanks to my family and friends for their unerring support and encouragement; to Gillian Levinson, whose kindness, patience and guidance made this story immeasurably better; to Ben Schrank, who was inspired enough to take a chance on a peculiar verse-novel for children; to Victor Rivas, whose artwork is always a gorgeous and humbling compliment to my words; to Jackie Kaiser, without whom I would be living out of (or possibly in) the trunk of someone else's car; to Kristin Smith, whose design work brings the freedom of poetry to life; and to Mitch Kowalski and everyone at the Toronto Writers' Centre, where my salvation is a room full of silent gray cubicles.

I would also like to thank that rascally philosopher-fool, Mulla Nasruddin. It was while reading one of his comic adventures that the seeds of Spud were sown.

Lastly, my deepest thanks to my beautiful, wonderful wife, without whom nothing happens. It's a mad roller-coaster we're on and the loops keep coming, but as long as I have you, let them.

IF YOU LOVE RHYMES
AND FAIRY TALES TOO,
THEN ONE OF THESE BOOKS
MAY BE JUST RIGHT FOR YOU . . .

★ "A natural descendant of the works of **Dr. Seuss** and **Roald Dahl** while hewing close to the droll atmospherics of **Edward Gorey** and **Lemony Snicket**." —*Booklist* (Starred; Top Ten Debut of 2008)

zorgamazoo

robert paul weston

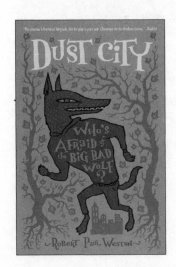

"This premise is fractured fairy-tale, but the glory is pure noir. *Chinatown* via the Brothers Grimm." –*Booklist*

DUST CITY

WHO'S AFRAID *of the* BIG BAD WOLF?

~ ROBERT PAUL WESTON ~